MAD
MANX
FURRY ROAD

George Gibson

First published by Stand Alone and Scream, 2015

An imprint of Gryphon Chess

This edition Copyright 2015, George Gibson

ISBN: 978-0-9943153-1-1

Sleeve design: C. Duryea

Character illustration: Chris Dirk

Copyeditor: Karin Angelika

Typeset in Palatino Linotype 11pt

This edition is printed in the United States of America

10 9 8 7 6 5 4 3 2 1

Contents

I: The Escape

Simmons struggled with the steering wheel, feeling every pain from the tracks and bare metal wheels up through to his knuckles.

"They're closing."

"Should've let me drive, Simmons," Manx mumbled as he chewed.

Simmons wiped the sweat beading down his whiskers.

A bullet whizzed past them.

The steering wheel jerked, Simmons grabbing it hard as the Interceptor's wheels smashed over scattered stones on the tracks.

"You just had to be a train today, dinya guvnor," Simmons whined. "How's we gonna find time to put the ruddy tires back on with that lot behind us?"

"You don't know my vehicle," Manx said.

"I gotta stop sleepin', mate; every time I do you bugga off and do somethin' stupid." Simmons glanced at the mirror to peer back down the tunnel. "Nuttun...where they gone? One minute they were there..."

Manx kept chewing and mumbled, "Thanks for waking up in time."

"What? Speak clear guv; what the hell are you eatin' anyway? Two mice at once?"

Manx thumbed the two wriggling tails hanging from his lips into his mouth, his cheeks bulging, and then he swallowed. "Mmmm…two-tailed Great Desert Skink," he said. "You should try."

"You always into eatin' on the run? You barely made it through the bloody sunroof, Manx. Those bastards were close. If I did'n' wake and warm up the donk, we'd be their meat, see?"

Manx said, "They say no one escapes the Ferals–"

"We escaped!" Simmon's wide-eyed brown and gray British Shorthair face puffed up as he held the vibrating steering wheel. "Now I can only hear our engine, so we lost 'em. And look, light at the end of the tunnel."

"I know my engine," Manx breathed. "It doesn't make *that* sound."

"What sound?"

A whistle shrilled through their ears.

"Nor that," Manx said. "Step on it."

"That's not the bogie-wheeled quad buggy that started chasing us," Simmons said.

A blinding light filled their cabin; something nudged them from behind, jolting them, their back wheels sparking.

"Christ it's a bloody steam train!"

"Told you it sounded different," Manx said coolly.

"They're right on top of us!" Simmons shrieked.

A bullet shrilled past, then another.

"Why you swipe that thing off 'em anyways?" Simmons asked, glaring at Manx who looked solemnly at the dirty silver panel in his hand. "Immodium Jack'll be real pissed. He'll shi' on our faces."

"It'll get me to Tailcutter."

"All this for Tailcutter?" Simmons scrunched his face. "All that effort to get the last locator from the Ferals and you still wan'ta find Tailcutter? I wan'ta find the Golden City."

"Sure they do too." Manx thumbed behind.

The Interceptor jolted on the tracks again.

Bullets shrilled past.

"Hand me the sawed-off."

Simmons passed him the gun.

Manx sat it over his shoulder, pointing behind him, while still looking forward. He tilted it out the window and fired one shot onto the tunnel wall behind them. He heard the ricochet whistle off the tunnel wall and ding onto the train.

Someone screamed above the roar of the steam engine bearing down on them.

"Damn," Manx said flatly.

"Whaddareyoudoing?" Simmons screeched. "You's gotta *aim!*"

Something thudded on the roof.

A fuzzy chalky-painted yellow-eyed cat wearing a leather muzzle bearing dingo canines grimaced down at them through the sunroof.

Manx bit his lip, held the gun in the same position and fired again. The sound shrilled off the tunnel wall and he heard a louder ding, followed by a hiss of steam swirling down the train.

More Ferals screamed over the venting steam.

Simmons groped for the intruder's flicking sawed-off. He grabbed something and gripped tight, realizing it was the arm of the Feral. He pulled down hard to hold it and flicked a switch up with his knee to slide the sunroof closed.

The gun clattered to the floor as the Feral above screamed, his arm spraying blood as the serrated edge of the sunroof closed in.

"Nice conversion, guv'na."

The Feral slid back across the roof, minus an arm. The arm landed on Simmons's lap and bled through his crotch.

"Fer frick's sake!"

"I really should be driving now," Manx said calmly.

Simmons held up the severed Feral arm and shook it, wiggling the paw. "Wanna hand?"

"I mean it." Manx narrowed his eyes.

"What? Now? You fureal?"

"I know that loco. They rigged a water cooled gas boiler. I hit the lap joints on the boiler; the box should blow any second. So hammer down."

The rear of the Interceptor lurched again, their back wheels sparking.

"Why haven't they fallen back?" Simmons asked.

"More shells, quick," Manx urged.

Simmons fumbled for the dropped gun as the back of their car suddenly seemed to lift off the tracks.

"They're goddamn pushing us!" Simmons yelled.

A bullet punched through the roof, skimming down the side of the door.

"Steam should've held them off," Manx said, "Something's wrong."

A rusted metal spike tore through the rear hatch area, ripping one of the tanks protruding through the windshield gap. Manx ducked, feeling the air go chilly around his ear.

The tank hissed and whistled, the gas venting behind them.

"Jeez Christ!" Simmons shrieked.

"Spare nitrous tank almost empty anyway," Manx said flatly.

"Bullet box, here," Simmons said.

The spike retracted and returned to slice through the metal below the rear tanks.

Manx reloaded.

"That's one mean loco coupling," Simmons cried.

Manx fired two more bullets at the Feral train. "Now…" He flicked his claw tips at Simmons. "The wheel."

"But–"

Manx reached for the dropped sawed-off and wedged it from the seat to the pedal.

"C'mon."

Simmons got up awkwardly from his seat as more bullets shrilled past him.

"Think they'll shoot the tires?"

Manx shook his head. "Idiot, we're on tracks."

"A joke, guvnor, a joke."

"Fine time." Manx slipped into the driver's bucket seat while Simmons slumped onto the passenger seat, upside down, paws and tail in the air.

A bullet whizzed past, nicking Simmons' tail.

"Shit, bloody shit!"

"You'll live."

"Easy for you, having no tail," Simmons cried.

"Here, take this." Manx handed Simmons the locator, and then reached under the dash to swing out a panel with a row of six toggle switches and LEDs. "You better belt up, Simmons." He flicked each one in a sequence; left two first, far right two next, middle two last.

The car jolted forwards; the rising shrill piercing their ears.

"Shiiiit!"

"Chill Simmons; that gas steam engine's far behind us," Manx said.

Simmons felt glued to the seat, still upside-down. "Wha-what was that?"

"Boost," Manx said. "And you don't drink it, unless you wanna be a Feral living in those tunnels back there under the ass of Immodium Jack."

The sunlight blinded them as they emerged from the tunnel, the tracks glinting into the distance.

"They'll be after us," Manx said quietly.

"Unless they blow," Simmons said.

A deep rumbling sound uttered from the mouth of the tunnel, smoke billowing outside.

"Yes!" Simmons said, making a fist.

"They'll still be after us," Manx said.

Something glinted in the light as it moved on the track ahead.

Their vehicle ka-thunked over a gap in the track; a metal sound rattled underneath them.

The vehicle thunked again.

"Shit," Simmons cursed.

Manx squinted as he looked in the mirror.

"You better slow down now, Manx."

"Shit," Manx cursed.

"They put us off the main track," Simmons said, the tone of his voice rising, "This one's about to run out."

Manx slammed the brakes, the screeching sound rippling across the desert and crackling back to their ears off distant hills.

A shower of sparks sprayed out behind them.

"How far?"

"What?" asked Simmons.

"How bloody far?"

"Another half mile, before the cliff edge."

"Cliff?" Manx glared at him. "Tiger nitrous needs room to brake; especially on train tracks. How deep's the cliff?"

Simmons scratched under his puffy chin. "Deep. And there are clowns down at the bottom. It's called Clown Chasm. Everyone knows it."

"That don't sound funny," Manx said flatly as he hammered the brakes.

"Wow, check the sparks behind us," Simmons gasped. "This section of rail ain't been used in years, it's all rusted."

The Interceptor's wheels screeched on the track as the vehicle slowly ground to a halt only a few yards from the cliff edge, the trailing smoke wafting past into the openness beyond.

Simmons let out a big sigh. "Phew, no clowns for us today, guvnor." He smiled.

Manx looked at him oddly. "Except back there." He kicked the door open.

Simmons struggled out and held his tail, wiping off the blood. "Yeah, I'll live...but it bloody hurts."

Manx ignored him as they walked to the cliff edge and looked down past the gnarled, twisted tracks that poked the air with severed ends.

"Looks steep," Manx said as he squinted to see the ruined railcars scattered across the bottom. Many were painted with pictures of clowns, their images partly covered in sand. Manx produced his monocular and extended it to see the writing on one of the cars. "Scow Circus... never heard of them."

"Ah...guvnor..." Simmons said slowly, his voice trembling. "We got a 'lil problem."

Manx stared down at the chasm as glimpses of his child and wife Josie flooded his vision, before being torn away as the scowls of Tailcutter's black and orange-painted face and the snipping of garden shears too hold.

Manx blinked hard.

"Manx!"

"What?"

Simmons pointed his paw. "Our 'lil problem..."

"Shit."

Out from the dusty swirls behind them emerged the Feral train.

Simmons took a deep breath. "How the 'ell?"

"Told you."

Manx casually slipped into the driver's seat and sat there.

"What you doin'?" Simmons screeched, waving his arms.

"Relax. Get in."

Simmons shrugged and climbed in. "Relax. Sure thing. Relax...I must bloody relax..."

"Shut up." Manx adjusted the mirror, watching the approaching train, steam billowing out the sides. A giant claw-like wedge plow appeared to emerge from a compartment mounted in front of engine.

"Where'd that bucker come from?" Simmons wailed, "They're gonna git us this time."

Manx sat there, eyeing the mirror as the train drew closer. He spotted the Ferals dancing on top of a railroad car behind the engine, their spears and rifles poking through the swirls of steam.

"Manx! Do something! It's getting real close!"

Manx remained seated, watching them in the mirror; he slowly pawed at his whiskers.

"Manx! C'mon!" Simmons opened the door and stuck a leg out.

Manx grabbed his arm and growled. "Get in."

"But–"

"Shut the door."

Simmons closed the door and sat there looking forward, his face gone white; he glanced at his side mirror. "That noise, that steam and thunder, I can still hear the Ferals screaming over the top of it."

The tracks vibrated under the car.

Manx flicked two switches under the dash.

Simmons scratched his right ear and slowly read the small labels above the switches, "Hy…drau…lic…Compression. What it do guv??"

From under the wheel arches another set of wheels groaned outwards. The wheels tilted down and clicked into the vertical position. Simmons looked out the door as he heard a sharp hissing.

"Inflating tires," Manx said.

"Shit boss, we're rising up."

The Interceptor lifted off the tracks. The inner track wheels retracted underneath.

Manx turned to Simmons and gave a half wry smile.

"Shit, I gotta stay awake more," Simmons said. "I wondered where you'd put the tires, guvnor." He looked behind as the locomotive closed in.

"Ahem, now guv?"

Manx waited, and then casually steered the Interceptor off the tracks, onto the desert floor.

The train swept past them, diving into Clown Chasm, barreling down the steep ragged slope and smashing into several pieces, the engine groaning and billowing a mix of steam and smoke from the furnace. It exploded amidst the screams and cries of Ferals. And then the gas chamber exploded, sending shards of metal into the sky above.

Manx stopped the car and gestured to Simmons. "Hand me the locator."

He got out and peered over the cliff edge.

"Stupid bastards."

He held the locator panel, licked his paw and rubbed the dirt off it. He tapped a silver power button; a screen flickered on and then faded.

A black shape in the corner of his eye caught his attention and he looked up. He squinted and then looked away.

Something grabbed his leg.

Manx toppled back as a Feral swung a knife to his leg, missing by inches.

The Feral pounced onto Manx, howling, its screams rippling through his ears, the wretched blue eyes and scarred face contorting.

Manx punched the Feral as they wrestled closer to the edge.

The Feral reached for a second knife on his belt, lifted it up and–

Simmons fired his rifle.

The wild cat fell back out of view, disappearing behind the cliff edge in a gurgling scream.

Simmons cupped his ear as he leaned over the edge.

Manx heard a thud and nodded.

"There, guv." Simmons puffed his chest up and released a big sigh. "Told you I'd save your life one more time."

"That's two. You need five for even," Manx said flatly as he got up and dusted himself.

"So that thing you stole, that locator. How you gonna make it work?"

"It's a TomTom," Manx said.

"Yeah, I know. So how's the hell you think one of those'll work? No power, and there in't no satellites no more. It's all gone in the Great Undoing. All gone Manx, all gone."

"This is the last," Manx said, holding it firmly in his paw. He looked to the sky. "And up there they told me there is one last camera satellite orbiting this dusty rock."

"Who told you? So how you power it then, ay? The car battery can't take no more juice being sucked."

Manx laughed. "Small current draw, but I won't use the battery. I stole the Stetson for power."

Simmons scratched his head.

"Let's get outa here, Simms."

They climbed into the Interceptor, Simmons shaking his head as he glanced at the gashed nitrous tank. "Why I stick..., why I stick with you..." he mumbled.

Manx revved the car and steered it away from the chasm. "We need high ground," he said. "There." He pointed.

"Gawdon bleedn' Bennett, no way," Simmons breathed, "Not Pride Mountain."

Manx winked and grinned mischievously. "Don't worry; she has no beef with me."

2: Rani Fluffiosa

The shadow from a nearby cliff touched the edge of the silver Interceptor as Manx leaned against the vehicle, fiddling with the silver panel, running a wire from the dark rat pelt Stetson on his head. He looked to the horizon, towards the mountain and tilted his hat. Dust kicked up in the distance. He examined the silver panel, the back pulled apart with wires hanging from it.

Simmons eyed Manx oddly and wondered why he would steal a wide-brim hat. "That's a whackjob head piece, Manx. You's a funny-looking cowboy cat in the hat."

Manx frowned. "Never heard of solar fabric?"

"Nup."

"Photovoltaics are interwoven into the rat pelt, using silver nitrate fractal tree nano-fibers. People used to wear solar clothes years before the Great Undoing. The tech uses peltier thermodynamics for heating or cooling; good all-terrain, all-condition clothing."

"Ooh, that old world talk, guvnor; shit you talk a lot. But it's still a bloody rat hat. Hope you keep a cool head."

"It'll power my TomTom," Manx said. "Need to charge it before going up the mountain."

"They'll see you."

Manx shrugged.

"Momma's got power, guns, and watchers everywhere. Bet 'em Ferals prolly think we's one of Momma's kittens.

And Momma may think we's Ferals. You sure you wanna go? Immodium Jack'll be roight behind us."

"They're probably too busy with the train wreck," Manx said quietly.

"Momma's a mean momma, guvnor. She'll be pissed 'cos you pissed off Immodium Jack. You know she got breeder slaves, all toms for her pussy harem, you be'r watch out. They'll put you in a duel, and if you lose you become a cook slave or even worse, working in the Tray. You'll starve. They say the only one's getting fat is Momma Cat."

Manx shrugged again. "Won't be there long. They don't go to the top of the mountain, they don't like the eagles." He eyed the dust swirl in the distance.

"Blimey not them Ferals again?"

"Dunno."

"We's go hide, in case?"

"Where?" asked Manx. "Open desert; they'll see our dust."

"Suppose you could take a dump in the desert an' the Ferals'll find it."

"Not Ferals." Manx held his monocular. His right whiskers twitched as he squinted to see. "Vehicles; turnpike doubles, triples...a convoy...not heading for us. But tells us where the road is so we can avoid the stinking plants. Let's go."

"You fureal?" Simmons yelled. "You crazy bastard!"

Manx climbed into the Interceptor.

"Why you always want trouble?"

"Get in, scaredy cat."

"Jeez," Simmons cursed.

"We need another nitro tank. They may have. We need tiger fuel. They may have. We need spare tire after that desert plant blowout. They may have."

Simmons rolled his big green eyes. "Sure they, whoever... *what*-ever they are, will hand it to us."

Manx turned the key.

The engine throbbed, the turbines whined and he tapped the accelerator. He drove off towards the distant dust swirl.

Simmons shook his head.

- - -

"Keep up with 'em," Cockflincher yelled. "Ya's letting 'em get away ya's frickun' mongrel!"

"The impellers need cleaning," said Spanky as he wiped his sweating brow. He pressed a few buttons and thumped an instrument dial on the dash. He hit both pedals in unison while changing gears.

The truck groaned. Dust flew up across their faces from the fleeing convoy ahead as a smoldering fuel barrel skipped down the road towards them before exploding.

"Whatta waste!" Spanky jerked the wheel and one of the toms further down the truck lost his footing, falling only to catch the handrail in time. "Bit hard trying to stay steady in all this shit, *and* get more power."

"Don' care, Spanky, keep this truck moving. An order. You's know orders. A bleedin' order, or Momma will be pissed."

"Yeah, at you, Cockfeltcher," Spanky yelled back. He rolled his big yellow eyes at the oversized white and gray tom standing there gawking at him, his body strapped in steel brake lines.

"I'm the engineer," Spanky said. "You're just the middle manager, with a middle finger that does the talking."

"One more time you mis-pronouncy me's name an' I'll cut yer bleedin' 'eart out."

Spanky flung his arm to the desert. "What's that?"

Cockflincher spotted the small dust haze coming towards the leading convoy. "Beats me. Maybe Rani's got some pals to help her." He grabbed the brass telescope mounted on a pivot on top of the tractor unit and focused to see the silver and black shape of the Interceptor leading the dust swirl. "Where I knows that X1 from?" he mumbled.

"Wookieepedia?" Spanky asked.

"Keep drivin', smartass," Cockflincher ordered.

- - -

Manx shifted gear and drove past the leading convoy. A bullet shrilled past them from the convoy behind.

"Not again," Simmons groaned. "Why bother? Too far; utter waste of bullets."

They pushed through the last dust swirl and Manx spotted a dozen ragged cat tribesmen caged on the back of a double-decker B-Train cargo trailer.

"Shit guvnor, converted cattle haul for toms," Simmons said.

The semi up ahead caught his eye and he accelerated.

"Pussy! A busload of pussy," Simmons gasped.

"Quiet."

One of the girls, a fiery red-furred cat leaned out of the rear compartment and let off a round. The bullet skipped off the Interceptor's hood with a warped whistling sound.

Manx accelerated past them and lined up the Interceptor with the lead vehicle to see a hybrid mix of bus and truck slapped together with added metal sheeting and rusted I-beams running down the sides to the thick grille guard.

The driver glanced at him; her startling blue-eyed rag doll half-smile and wild hair caused Manx to swerve.

She poked a double barrel through the window past her ginger passenger.

Manx swerved again.

Simmons ducked.

The catgirl fired both rounds.

Manx pressed the accelerator.

"Jeez you bloody wanna get us killed matey!" Simmons shrieked.

"Getting in front," Manx said with a growl in his voice.

The ginger passenger poked her big round face out of the window and yelled, "Piss off; we're not going back to Momma."

"Not with Momma," Manx yelled.

Simmons crouched, covering his ears.

"Boolsheet!" Both catgirls hissed.

"Serious."

"Prove it," yelled the ginger passenger.

Manx stared at both of them for a moment and then swung off the road, spinning the vehicle about in a donut before correcting it and driving off towards the rear of the first convoy.

"You'se stinkin' mad, Manx. Whaddya gonna do guv? Whaddya gonna do?"

"Stop the other convoy," Manx said flatly.

"Stop the… oh frick off surely!" Simmons nursed his tail. "Spose you can't stop now an' let me out, guv'?"

"Nah," Manx said flatly.

He slammed the accelerator and raced back down the convoy line. Girls in the other trucks waved and jeered at them as they passed, one firing a bullet that whistled by, nicking the side mirror.

"Charming," Simmons said indignantly. "Back in the 'ol country we'd not get that sort o' behavior."

"World Die, the Great Undoing or whatever you want to call it is done," Manx said. "There's just here and that's it."

"What about the Golden City? It's the last city ever."

"You believe those Ferals?"

"Everyone talks of it, even Momma. It's on the coast," Simmons said.

"Which coast? The Risen?"

"Yeah, the new coast."

"It's *all* new coast."

"It's there, I know it is. I was glad when you went looking for the locator. I know you want to go there too. Forget Tailcutter, he's gone, along with your childhood. Hope is the new city."

"Hope is shit."

"I tell you guv, we is wastun' our time with this lot."

Manx ignored him and sped the Interceptor past the last triple-trailer, heading for the pursuing convoy in the distance.

- - -

"Hey Cockafella, we catchin' up, or is that something approaching us up ahead?"

"That don't da look right, Spanky," he replied stupidly. Cockflincher shoved his hand down his pants and adjusted himself.

Spanky shook his head.

"It's big, right? It's big. Momma's so impressed."

Spanky looked away. "Yeesh."

"It's that desert vehicle again," Cockflincher grumbled.

"We're getting close," Simmons said.

Manx slammed the brakes midway and spun the rear so that it faced the approaching convoy. He flicked a lever and oil began to ooze onto the road. "Let's give 'em the slip."

Simmons rolled his eyes. "Shit guvnor, I always wanted to say that. Just like Bond. And he had an Interceptor too."

"That was a Jensen, douche."

Manx held the handbrake up and revved the car. The tires spun, spewing blue smoke into the air, and then he flicked another switch to jettison a canister of fuel that broke apart when it hit the asphalt. He fired a bullet into it. He released the handbrake and hammered the pedal to speed back towards the leading convoy. The fuel and oil behind them ignited and began to burn across the road as it spilled.

Manx raced the Interceptor away while Simmons twisted his neck to see behind. "You got Kumho tires? Shit man."

"Jeez," Spanky said. "Do we drive through this? So much blue smoke.... Can't see...I gotta brake."

"No, Spanky. Look... Kumho blue, rool pretty," Cockflincher said slowly.

"Snap out of it Cockflogger; it's that's other smoke I don't like, and the road's burning."

Cockflincher grabbed a rag-covered microphone and yelled, "Lower the skid ramps. Johoks go!"

Two metal ramps swung down onto the road, either side of the semi, clanking and sparking, as a dozen fat-faced motorbike cats in wide dirty-orange hockey masks and rifles slung over their shoulders, raced down onto the asphalt, arcing their bikes into the desert to turn and ride off around the smoke and head for the leading convoy. Their orange wedge-furhawks glinted in the low sun as they rode off chanting, "Gimmi-gimmi-gimmi...."

"I can't brake in time!" Spanky pressed the pedal hard and the truck lurched, skidding and then sliding across the burning oil.

"Jump, ya bastards!" Cockflincher yelled.

The semi tipped over on its side, groaning and sparking as it slid across the fiery road.

The trucks and buggies behind screeched to a halt as the Interceptor disappeared over the horizon, the Johoks in pursuit.

- - -

Manx swung his Interceptor in front of the lead truck.

The catgirl driver swerved their massive semi-trailer, nudging the grill guard against his mangled fender.

He padded the brakes, as they honked from behind and he watched them slow, hearing the air brakes hissing.

Manx flung his arm out and waved them off the main road to follow down a dirt trail some distance.

The rag doll leapt from the tractor unit, waving two sawed-off guns. Her ginger friend followed, packing a slightly smaller piece with a long magazine jutting underneath the barrel.

"How dare you!" yelled the rag doll.

"A thank you would be nice," Manx said flatly.

"I'm the Rani, and you, idiot, are now my prisoner. You can join the toms in the cattle-haul."

Two more soldiers jumped from the other trucks as they came to a stop.

One of them, a tall Russian Blue covered in leather straps and studs dragged a kicking Simmons out of the Interceptor. "What you want with this cute one, boss?"

Simmons opened his mouth.

Manx frowned and nodded sideways to him.

"So who the frick are you?" Rani asked.

"Manx Rockytabby. And this is my spare wheel, Simmons.

"Arthur Shorthair Simmons," he said quickly.

Rani suddenly let out a raucous howl-like laugh. "Manx. You're a tabby, named Manx!"

"Ah, Max actually, but I lost my tail as a kitten to that token-loving marauder Tailcutter, and everyone's called me Manx ever since."

"It's cute," said the ginger girl.

"Meet my half sis', Magazine Madonna," Rani said, flicking her arm casually at the large ginger cat, "Otherwise known as 32 Round Maggie."

"Not that it means I'm *that* round," she said quickly and giggled. "Just call me Maggie."

"Hmm, great family resemblance," Manx said with a half-smile.

Rani ignored him. "And this is Gertrude, my aide."

Gertrude stood tall, gripped her piece and smirked at them.

"Don't worry; all Russian Blues are like that."

Manx huffed.

Simmons observed Maggie's gun and hissed. "Shit, guv, double-grip Intratec," he said under breath. "How's she hold that heavy piece of crap?"

"I'm in the mood for grip, Simmy," Maggie said, winking at him.

"Where'd you get all this?" Manx asked, looking at all the weapons they held.

The other girls, dressed as leather-and-metal-clad soldiers, suddenly stood legs apart, lifting their rifles up at Manx and Simmons.

Manx reached for his sidearm.

"Keep your weapons," Rani said as she flicked her hand at the girls. "Compliments, Momma Cat."

"Compliments," Manx said flatly.

"She's mean, that Momma. Compliments, as in stolen," Simmons said.

"Ah so you know her, Simmy boy."

Simmons gulped.

"You're fine," Rani said, laughing. "Momma prefers bigger fish."

Simmons went red in the face and Manx sneered at him.

"But you," Rani said, running her claws lightly over the fur on Manx's upper chest, "Would make her very happy indeed. I hope you weren't going to see her, when she's done, she'll rip you apart."

"Told you we shouldn't go to Pride Mountain," Simmons hissed.

Manx glared at him.

Rani placed paws on hips. "You must be kidding."

"Just like the view on top of the mountain," Manx said carefully.

Rani laughed again, her fluffy head catching the light; her big blue-steel ragdoll eyes gave a mocking look.

"Those eagles will tear you apart too, not to mention shit on your face at the same time. No one goes to Pride Mountain unless they are looking… for a *signal*." She motioned to the soldiers. "Search their car."

Two soldiers rummaged through the Interceptor, hissing and spitting, tossing bullet cases and clips aside. One shook her head sideways.

Rani drew close to Manx, her paw drawing down his chest and inside his leather jacket.

Manx stopped her paw as she stared into his deep eyes. He felt something prod him in the groin and he looked down slowly. The end of her sawed-off nudged his crotch as she eased the silver TomTom from his jacket. She held it up and grinned, the sun glinting in her canines. "My-my, haven't seen one of these for a lonnng time. You were gonna either trade with Momma, or go signal hunting," She said. "I think the latter."

"Doesn't work," Simmons said.

A bullet shrilled over their heads.

They looked around and back towards the road but could see nothing.

With a clatter of stones, motorbikes launched from the shallow cliffs above.

One rider flew over the top of them; the furhawk biker, wearing a rusty-colored hockey mask, swung his gun down and fired.

Manx swiped the TomTom from her and grabbed Simmons by the shoulder.

They scampered for the Interceptor.

"Johoks!" Maggie yelled. "That means Cockflincher will be upon us."

"What's a Johok, guv?"

"A Hokean tribescat. They're hardly loyal to anyone, greedy bastards, raping and stealing. They have a chant, *'gimmi-gimmi-gimmi'*. Can't you hear 'em? Dunno why they're working for Momma."

"This is your fault," Rani shouted as she ducked another bullet.

Manx crouched behind the Interceptor and then dropped to the ground next to Simmons as more bullets rained upon them. He peered up to count eleven riders.

A rider flew overhead from a rocky rampart behind them, swinging his rifle down and firing.

Maggie dodged the ground-skipping bullets.

Simmons fired at the Johok, knocking the gun out of its hand but the Johok landed on both wheels and spun about. Screeching and revving, the rider launched his bike back over the top of the Interceptor and Manx shot a round into the back of his modified wheel hub helmet; cat separating from bike mid-flight.

"Gear up, we're leaving!" Rani cried.

"But I want Simmy, that shorthair snout," Maggie wined.

Rani tugged her paw. "Cockflincher will get us and take us back to Pride Mountain. Let's *go*." She jerked Maggie away as bullets skipped the ground, popping dust in the air in their wake.

"Gimmi-gimmi," screamed another Johok biker as he jerked his rear wheel to make a crude donut before them.

Rani fired a round into his face. The biker's cheeks split apart in a splash of blood.

The Johok gawked at her before falling backwards, bike and rider slumping to the ground.

Manx thumbed his pocket for a couple of rounds and cocked his gun. He peered at the mêlée beyond the Interceptor. "They don't look concerned with us, just the man-train cattle-haul back there, Simmons. They want the cargo. Shit, see that? Rani's taken. Big dude with something packed down his pants."

Manx looked down at Simmons who remained still, crouching against the Interceptor door.

"Simmons."

"*Simmons!*" Manx nudged him.

Simmons slumped over; mouth agape, blood streaming from his forehead.

Simmons was dead.

Manx gulped. He slowly closed the British shorthair's eyelids over his fading green eyes. He clenched his paws and looked through the dirty Interceptor glass to see the trucks departing, the riders giving chase, as more vehicles from the other convoy arrived. He fell back and whacked his head against the door. He whacked it again, and again, and bit his lip.

He heard the fading sounds of trucks and bikes take off into the distance, and he wiped his brow.

"Shit."

3: Desert Meanderings

Manx clenched the wheel and stared ahead, ignoring the smeared windshield. The road was smooth in the moon glow, almost shiny, he thought. He gazed into the distant night, and counted a dozen stars above the hazy dark horizon. He recalled when he met Simmons, at a gas station while under attack by rogue police stealing fuel. The scenes fled past him, how Simmons reluctantly took the spare rifle from him and found the courage to fire at the rogue cops while everyone else was pinned down. Simmons hadn't needed to use a gun until that day.

"He saved my sorry life," Manx mumbled. "All I did was treat him like a thorn in my boot ever since."

Tailcutter's grimace then flooded his mind, sending him back to his childhood, the shears clacking as Tailcutter gawked at him; all screw-faced and menacing towards the timid kitten, while announcing, *"It's trophy time, my little cub."* Manx screamed a kitten scream that day but the agony was even more painful as he watched Mom and Pop hand over his severed tail to Tailcutter in exchange for food, before passing out, only to wake and see Tailcutter slitting their throats upon the slightest of protests.

The scene burned into his mind and he shoved it aside for the road ahead of him, until the crackling demise of his wife Josie and child flooded his vision, playing out again and again; how Tailcutter knew where they were hiding, how he knew where she would be, how the fire raged so fast.

And then he thought of Rani, and Maggie, and the Ferals, and wondered about Momma Cat. Momma has them, he mused. Momma has them.

Manx stared into the night, and the long road into blackness to who-the-frick knows where anyway, he thought. Simmons was right, Tailcutter is probably long gone. He'd be old now, more rancid and wiry, and no doubt just as crazed. Or he'd be dead at the hand of someone else.

The faded road markers seemed to slide underneath him, his vision going blurry, the road appearing like a huge asphalt tongue, swallowing him into something bad beyond. But it didn't matter. Losing a wife, child, and parents; it all became a racing blur. Shit happens everywhere, he acknowledged, I can be part of it, or be part of nothing.

He slammed the brakes, drifting the car about as he reined the handbrake tight, letting it go slowly to point the car in the opposite direction. A cloud of dust passed the windshield and he stared blankly down the road he had just come down. He waited and stared, sweat beading down his forehead.

He floored the pedal, spinning the wheels, and took off into the night, back towards Pride Mountain, back to a different kind of darkness, just as incalculable, perhaps more menacing – probably more stupid. He raced over the shallow rises, expecting perhaps someone to be waiting for him; every rise led to another stretch of black road. He approached to where they left the road earlier. He swept past the hastily thrown-together mound of rocks that covered Simmons. He kept the pedal down and kept driving as the stars shifted in the sky. He swept past the silhouette of a rolled semi-trailer by the side of the road. He fixed his stare straight ahead and murmured, "More shit. But shit I can deal with."

- - -

Rani looked about the cattle haul. She squirmed under her leather bindings, tossing her head back to flick off the annoying rag doll curls. She barked at Maggie, "You held me up. It's all your fault."

"So not; it was that Manx dude."

"Sure. As soon as you saw Momma's cats coming up behind us, you capitulated real easy."

"Cockflincher–"

"I don't wanna hear no more, Maggie. You never wanted to leave Pride Mountain, I suspected it, now I know it. You just like size, not brains."

"Cockflincher's not my type, but Simmons–"

"Enough!"

A tom in shackles threw up beside her and she kicked him away.

"Momma's not going to be pleased with you," Maggie said.

The cattle-haul clanked and juddered as it sped down the road towards a distant mountain looming up from the horizon.

"I'm the Rani," she said. "How dare they put me here with breeder toms."

"Momma sees you as shit, Fluffiosa, a fake leader," Maggie said.

"But you were *with* me," Rani said. "I thought you wanted to go to a better place. All this breeding stock for little kitty soldiers? She picked a poor lot here. Some are Ferals."

"Speak for yourself," someone mumbled in the shadows. "We work hard for Momma. You should know what she has us really do."

A bullet rang off the steel cage.

Rani glared into the shadows and then looked up to see the silhouette of a soldier, and in the moon-light she wondered who had betrayed her.

"Gertrude!" she yelled.

Rani stared at the silhouettes standing above the cattle cage, the shape of their guns, the bulging leathers, wide belts and serrated knives – all soldiers. She squinted to see into the darkened faces of the tom prisoners around her, and she could not see a captured soldier. She eyed Maggie. "You think what I think?"

Maggie nodded. "We been done in."

"Not again."

"Wonder what Cockflincher offered them?"

"Their lives?"

Another bullet shrilled past.

"Silence," someone screeched above them.

The cattle-haul jolted again. The cage rattled and the vehicle lurched over uneven ground. Some of the toms groaned. Another threw up. They must not have eaten anything for a while, Rani thought.

"Not far now; we're at Fur Ridge," Maggie said. "They're going the direct route, not our escape route, they mustn't know 'bout it."

"It's getting worse," Rani whispered. "The asphalt crinoids will have eaten this section of the road completely in another year or so."

"Momma's got a problem," Maggie said. "How will she trade fuel and water for tom breeds with those northern tribes if the road gets eaten by the wandering plants?"

"She'll wanna know our escape route. You better not tell her," she urged.

Maggie sighed. "I just want my DC9 back."

Rani leaned on her shoulder and closed her eyes. "Forget about that stupid gun. Get some rest, you'll need it."

- - -

His head dropped, the car wavered. He flicked open his deep amber eyes and caught a hint of sunlight edging the hilly horizon in a jagged string of red. Manx released a loud gravelly yawn and wondered how he had made it this far without falling asleep, let alone farting, which he would have blamed Simmons for. His heart leapt and he struggled to push all the violent memories aside. He leaned forward, trying to scope the shapes on the road ahead, which seemed to move.

The vehicle jolted over something. An image of running over Tailcutter immediately came to mind and he smirked.

The vehicle bumped and jolted again and then a dash panel light flashed red before him. The Interceptor gurgled and choked and Manx throttled down as he tapped the fuel gauge. He cursed himself for not replacing the light bulb behind the dial. The Interceptor bounced over the lumpy surface and Manx spotted the tapering yellow fronds of the road crawlers, mounded up in clumps and scattered haphazardly across the asphalt.

His vehicle spluttered to a halt and moments later the tabby timer shut down, the whine dropping off to the silence of the breeze, and the sounds of the thick yellow desert fronds brushing their spikes against his tires.

Manx struggled outside and opened the trunk for the spare jerry can to see a gaping hole in its side, the lingering stench of tiger fuel making him cough. He then wondered why they hadn't smelt it earlier. He cursed under breath, and grabbed the handle and lobbed the can off the side of the road.

He expected a clanging noise but the muffled bumpy sounds made him look further away. Across the desert floor, the rising sun lit a yellow glinting sea of fronds, all bowing gently in a slight breeze. He looked to the hills and caught the shadow of a larger shape beyond, which he presumed was Pride Mountain.

"Frick!" He screamed. "Frick you bastards!"

He fell back against the Interceptor, his legs sliding onto the road as he slumped onto the asphalt.

Something dug into his side. He probed his jacket and produced the silver TomTom. He stared at it blankly and then pressed the power button. Expecting nothing, he watched the screen flicker on; a dozen colored squares appeared, and then the screen filled with the image of a coastline in full daylight. He thumbed the screen, and a network of roads appeared, and what looked like a city, in an almost uniform radial pattern, surrounded by water. The screen dithered, the shapes grew blocky and then the screen blanked out.

Manx tipped his head back against the Interceptor door and looked to the morning sky. He dropped the locator and fell asleep.

4: Momma Cat

Narrow chalky walls lined the stone-strewn winding road that snaked up the chasm to Pride Mountain. Rani opened her eyes slowly and groaned, before pushing Maggie off her lap. She eyed the toms, shackled in the cage with her, their gnarly unkempt faces blankly staring through gray eyes to the rough wooden floor. She knew they wouldn't look at her, even though someone in the cage last night had spoken up for a moment. None of them were like Manx or Simmons. Men here are useless, she thought, and maybe Momma Cat's right, they are good for stock and heavy work, and that's all.

The convoy slowly drove under a high rocky arch towards the Lair, on a road cobbled in semi-smooth stones, probably from a river that ran here hundreds of years ago, Rani had often thought. She looked up to see the familiar Screaming Skull, poorly-carved out from the mountain face, gawking high above them to the valley beyond. She spotted the massive rotund ginger cat looking down upon them from the gaping mouth at the Tooth Terrace; the furry breast leaned over the smoothed incisor fence, pressing folds of fur over the sides, and smirked at the weary travelers.

"Momma looks pissed," Maggie said.

"Duh, Mad Maggie. We tried to escape, and," Rani said, eyeing the soldiers, "it seems anyone can be bought."

The trucks stopped. Cockflincher, covered in scratches and road rash, stood atop the prime tractor unit and bellowed up to the cat skull. "We got'em Momma Cat, jus' as Oi said we would."

"Bring them," echoed Momma's voice.

The leather and harness-clad catgirl soldiers unloaded the cattle-haul and goaded the toms out with cattle prods.

One soldier grabbed Rani's arm.

Rani spat at her and uttered, "Next time, know your true leader, or die."

The white-leather-clad soldier's blue eyes widened and she stepped away, saying under breath, "Momma comes first."

She flicked her arm at two soldiers. "To the Lair with them."

Maggie watched the toms trudging in behind them, taken to the lower levels as they approached the yellow arched entry doors to Momma's lair.

Two tall black cat sentries swung open the creaking double doors.

The soldiers clapped their paws onto Rani and Maggie, shouldering them up to Momma, who sat sprawled across a great frayed red silk cushion, her massive ginger tail flicking the air. She ignored them, and continued to watch the big cracked screen hanging on the rocky wall above them, as a lizard tail flicked and disappeared into her mouth.

Rani and Maggie eyed each other and then sighed. They knew this was Momma's favorite archive footage.

Momma's tongue started to sag as she drooled at the scene of Fleaberaci the Birman playing the piano, singing,

"Oh Randy,

"Well you kissed me and stopped me

"From marking,

"And I need you today,

"Oh Randy…"

…Fleaberaci turns to the camera, smiles and says, "I wish my brother Barry was here," and then he winks–

"Oh…" groaned Momma.

The screen flickered and went black.

Momma grabbed a metal cone on a flex conduit tube hanging above her. She yelled into it, "Who's cut the power now? I wan' it back, 'yo hear, I wan' it back *nowwwwh!*"

"Sorry ma'aaam," she heard the scratchy voice reply through the tube, "The artesian water rush is flooding Turbine Four on the bottom level again. And they are hard to repair since you banished Jock–"

"Just fix it! And seal all those bulkheads. Remember what Immodium Jack and his Ferals did last time."

Momma leaned towards Rani and Maggie, her fur bulging through the many belts and harnesses that crisscrossed her frame. Her big turquoise eyes widened. "So, wayward pussies," she bellowed, "how in this dusty hell could you think you could undermine me by taking my prized toms and leaving me?" She slowly shook her puffed up head. "Momma disappointed. Momma not happy with you." She motioned to a guard. "Take the Magazine Madonna."

"Hey!" Maggie shook herself free.

Momma narrowed her eyes to slits and bared her teeth. "Just because you're my big mature daughter, doesn't mean you're ready to go on a little adventure of your own."

"She wasn't on her own," Rani protested. "And I'm your first daughter. And you don't let me do *anything*."

"Yes I do," Momma said, grinning. "I *let* you escape. Resistance is fertile, it gives you strength. You know you need to be here, to pick a sire."

"Bull."

Momma smiled, and bared her incisors. "Not true; you can choose any tom I have."

"Hah!" Rani laughed. "You just want to keep control."

Momma's smile dropped. "Take both of them to their rooms and lock the doors."

Maggie huffed.

The soldiers jerked the two girls about and led them away.

Rani glared at her soldiers. "So...all's a game, ay? And we get grounded anyway. How boring. This place is going to shit and no one listens. Wouldn't think of this shit coming from you, Gertrude."

The tall, slender Persian soldier leaned to her ear and whispered, "Patience."

Maggie eyed Rani and shook her head very slightly, and moved her lips without speaking.

Rani knew the words she mouthed:

"This is a game too."

5: Immodium Jack

"He's dead," said the Johok. The leather-clad wirehair tom kicked the leg of the slumped cat. "Oi; you stupid gray tiger."

Manx dropped to one side.

"This tabby ain't dead, Nad," said the other Johok as he scratched under his puffed up orange bobtail. "Dere's no flies yet. An' where's da blud? An' shit, look, where's his tail? He's loike me."

"Nah, Errol," said Nad. "Dis looks loike Tailcu'her's 'andy work." He stood up and examined the Interceptor. "Noice ve-hicle, Errol," he said as he kicked the tires. "I sure's could ditch moi roide for this."

"Nah, eats jooce, see?" Errol sniffed the jimmy-opened fuel door. "Nuttun'. Notta whiff."

"Pity, we could'ave 'ad an easy roide back to Momma." Nad spat on his paw and combed back his fluffed up furhawk. "He must'ave bin doin' some sirrious drivun, this bloke. Cor, I roolly like this car. Bet the donk is good."

Manx groaned and then coughed. His eyes remained closed as he mumbled, "Yeah, the donk's good."

"Shit, you see dat, Nad?"

Nad mounted his bike and rode up alongside the Interceptor fuel door and pulled a rubber hose and pump from his frayed backpack. He struggled to turn the fuel lid on the bike and spat on the ground as he wrenched it off.

He fed the hose into his bike, the other into the Interceptor fuel inlet and then he flicked a switch.

Errol lifted Manx upright and spat in his face. "Oi, piece of shit tabby. Wakey wakey."

Manx drew a deep slow breath and kept his eyes closed as he felt the close stink-breath of the tom warm his face. He guessed it was a Johok; nothing else could stink like shit and rotting milk at the same time. He flung his eyes open and lunged for the Johok's throat and gripped it hard and glared into the dirty cat's face.

Nad watched the tightening paw dig into Errol's neck as Manx extended his claws into the rough fur.

"Ooh, he's all tough," Nad barked before he brass knuckled Manx across the face, producing a splay of blood.

Manx slumped to the ground.

"Took ya time," Errol said, gasping while holding his neck. He looked to the ground beside Manx. "'Ere, wha's this?" He picked up the locator.

Nad laughed. "Shit, not see one of those foer while. Givvit a shake."

Errol scrunched his face up at the device while scratching beneath his whiskers. He shook it, and then flung it off the road.

Nad tightened the fuel cap on his bike and wheeled it off the road. "Mount up, Errol, I'll drive this four-wheeled X1 beast back to Momma. She'll be rool pleased."

"Aw why can't I drive?"

Nad growled at Errol, baring all his jagged teeth. With hands on leather-clad hips he watched Errol reluctantly mount his aged Ducati.

"Whaddabout your boike?"

"Tank's empty now, furwit. It's the last jerkin' Yamahahahah I'll ever roide."

"You's jus' don' look after your boikes, Nad. "Whaddabout him?" Errol pointed.

"Leave 'im to da dingos."

Errol sat on his bike and watched Nad swear and curse in the Interceptor, until finally starting the vehicle in spurts before throttling up.

Both car and bike then weaved their way slowly through the hundred yards or so of broken asphalt and lumpy yellow plants before the valley rang out with the sounds of their screeching wheels, signaling they had reached the clear part of the open road. Errol took off on his back wheel, and the Interceptor left a blue haze, as they headed back to Pride Mountain.

Manx lay unconscious, slumped on the road, as the wedge-tailed eagles and ravens circled high above.

- - -

The light danced across the tunnel walls, caused by the water funneling down to the pond before them. Feral screeches bounced around the walls in the shadows.

A large white tom, crisscrossed in chains and belts, lifted his skull muzzle and scratched his jaw underneath. He glanced down upon the slain Ferals at his feet and looked up to the others, narrowing his eyes, watching their collective eyes gleaming yellow, green, and blue in the semi-darkness, under the shimmering brick dome of the old sewer where the tunnels intersected.

He farted.

The cats blinked, some shuddered, but none moved.

"Gooood," breathed Immodium Jack. He farted again. "No one will dare run from me." He breathed in heavily, sucking in the musty stench of the tunnels. "What you did tudday was stewpid." He pointed his paw at the slain Ferals before his feet. "And these were particularly stewpid. We needed that loco. Now we are down to one."

"But they had rail wheels, master," a black and blotchy gray Feral said, his voice shaking.

"Tailbutt," Immodium breathed, "high praise for your inessstimable observation as usual. Nice kitty... But you miss the point. They wrecked my loco and took my locator. They took my only connection with civilization ...out there."

"Momma?" asked another Feral, scratching his wiry head.

"Stupid moggy! She has the locator and we need it back. They'll be leaving the mountain soon."

"Why?" asked Tailbutt. "She has power, and toms, and tommy guns, and... and luxury –and a telly. Why would she leave?"

"You know why, my sweet 'lil orange-eyed scruffball. The water is rising... everywhere... up from underneath." He shook his head. "I hate water; especially salty water. We need fresh water; we need supplies, and the locator."

"What about our tunnels to skulk about in," said an old wiry cat standing in the shadows, "and our old railway terminus, and equipment. An' lotsa rats an' cottontails to eat. Here is pretty good."

Immodium hissed. "We're *nothing* without pure water." He released an elongated fart, lifting his leg to one side as he balanced on the other leg and flicked his tail.

"Ahhhhhh...." The fart whined, the sound bouncing off the chamber ceiling. "Those tunnel rats don't agree with me."

The Ferals began to howl in unison. The tunnels resonated with their cries.

"Tailbutt, any gut pills left in the medicine cabinet?"

"Nothing, master, we're completely out."

Immodium belched and loosened the tatty belt around his bulging waist as another fart groaned and then squealed through the murky air. "Then it's toime to leave. First stop's for supplies. I's want new food, not rancid rats 'n three-eyed cottontails. I's want fuel, cars, boikes an' semis. And I's want da wimmen, allll da wimmen." He growled and screeched. "I's want what's at Momma's mount'in."

6: Desert Secret

He felt the pressure from above as they pounced on him, pinning him down. The clacking sound continued and he howled but all he could hear was laughter. The cold from the rock beneath him seemed to chill through his lungs as he gasped for air. He kicked furiously, flicking his tail as the gruff voice close to his ear told him to quit squirming. He felt the big dirty paw grip around the back of his neck and through his ears rang the screeches of other cats nearby, jeering, yelling for Tailcutter to do it now.

The screeching rang louder and Manx flung his eyes open to see a raven on his knee.

"Frick off!"

The bird sat there.

He jerked his knee and waved his arms about as the pain in his jaw intensified. The bird crapped near his crotch as it flew off.

Manx gripped his face, probed around the jawline and squeezed it tight, moving it about, feeling a clicking sound in the bone. He sat awkwardly upright, wiping blood off his paw on the road as he looked about. The desert fronds waved in the morning breeze. He spotted the ditched motorbike, and a glint off the road of something; the jerry can. He breathed hard, gasping as he felt the warming sunlight take the edge off the sharpness of the air, warmer with every breath.

Dizzy, he fell back onto a spiky yellow desert frond, thinking fleetingly that it was soft; only to find out it was just as sharp as desert spinifex. He looked about and scoped many old tires scattered about and thought how bad it was to drive over spinifex in the desert, but this plant was just as bad, maybe worse and he wondered how his car could have gotten this far. While lying on his side he examined the frond, the spikes tapering downwards, wrapped around a large bulb. He pulled at the plant and it lifted easily; he could see the roots had penetrated the asphalt which crumbled off in flakes as he lifted it higher. He then noticed the asphalt all cracked and crumbly around the base of each plant. He ripped apart one of the spiked bulbs and tore each spike off. He rubbed the bulb on the undamaged part of the road to smooth it. He held it to his mouth and bit into it.

The taste burned his throat and frothed up through his nose and he spat it out. He gripped his neck, his throat feeling coated by the stinging sap.

"Useless frickin' thing," he cursed.

He got up awkwardly and staggered to the abandoned motorbike and heaved it upright. He eyed the filthy tank bag hanging loose on sodden partly-ripped twine. He probed through the pockets; a roach ran out across his hand. He ignored it and produced a roll of duct tape which he pocketed. And then he felt the cold of a water bottle and pulled it out. It was a metal can with a cat skull logo. He whisked off the lid and hesitated before swallowing the contents.

He drank and drank and wiped his mouth. "Phew, it's not piss," he muttered as he gasped for air, after drinking it all in one go.

He wiped his mouth again and mounted the Yamaha and turned the key. A whine uttered from the dash.

"Been a long time frickwit," he cursed to himself. He spotted the plunger and pressed it, turned the key again, kicked down and throttled up.

The bike spluttered. He kicked down again. Nothing. The handlebar dash was covered in cracks and there was a hole where the fuel gauge was supposed to be. He reached through the hole and probed, feeling for the dial. He pulled it out along with a bunch of stubbed-out cigarette butts. He coughed from the stench. The dial showed Empty.

"Bastard bogans," he cursed.

He dismounted and looked to the horizon to see the mountain he guessed was where they went. He staggered forward, and then started to walk upright and more briskly before suddenly stopping and slowly turning around to see the plant-strewn road, broken-away asphalt and the abandoned bike. The glint of the jerry can caught his eye again. He returned to the bike and probed the tank bag, producing a match. He struck it against the asphalt where it lit instantly and he dropped it on the spat-out sap from the plant. The sap instantly ignited. He stomped his boot down, strode off the road and picked up the jerry can.

He clanged the can on the asphalt, on its side, hole facing down, and rubbed the can on the road to smooth the edges, ignoring the small spark puffs of fuel vapor. He then bit into the roll of duct tape, stretching out lengths from his teeth which he used to cover the hole. Forgetting about how much water he drank, he picked up the flask and sucked the wet air out of it.

He got up, sat the jerry can upright and flicked back the cap. He stood over the yellow frond bulb that had burned into his mouth and he picked a few more, stripped their spikes and jammed the ends into the can. He squeezed hard, pressing the juice into the jerry can.

The eagles circled overhead. A raven swooped past him.

He squeezed more bulbs into the can and took it to the bike.

"Shit," he said as he tugged on the fuel cap, trying to twist it open as pain ran through his paws. He stood up, feeling dizzy and weak.

He eyed the fuel cap and saw that the lock had been drilled in the center. Two holes were on either side of the keyhole and he picked up two spinifex spikes, snapped their ends off and sunk them in the holes, holding both together as he tried to twist off the cap. He gritted his teeth. The lid was jammed tight. He pressed his paws down around the spikes, feeling the cap budge underneath before coming loose. He took in a deep breath, unscrewed the cap, and flung it off.

He poured the frond juice into the gas tank while eyeing the eagles and ravens circling overhead.

A raven cawed, swooping low.

Manx ducked and gave it the finger. "Yeah up yours too, mutha."

The bird screeched again.

This time Manx thought he heard the raven say, "Nevermorrrrre..."

Manx replaced the fuel cap, tightening it with the two spikes, thinking they would make great short range darts and wondered if they would work on his crossbow, and then he spat on the ground as he thought of the weapon in the trunk of the Interceptor.

He ripped the tank bag off and duct-taped the jerry can to the back of the Yamaha. He mounted and hesitated before turning the key. The bike spluttered and groaned and he revved the motor, thinking it sounded more like a lawnmower.

Thoughts of his wife Josie returned. With every rev, a new memory blurred his vision. He made a slow start, weaving past the yellow asphalt-eaters, and then revved up and skidded off for Pride Mountain.

- - -

"Why's she keepin' us here?" Maggie asked.

Rani kicked the heavy metal door and clenched her fuzzy fists. "Don't know; it's not the first time we have crossed Momma. But this is different. We can't keep being played like this."

"Well I'm only a half daughter," Maggie said. "Wonder what your Rag poppa would have said."

Rani rolled her eyes. "Meh. Probably nothing. He was under the paw of Momma for years. Wish I knew where he took off to. It's been years now."

"Prolly better off dead," Maggie said. "Like my stinking ginger Pa."

The door clanged and they heard the bolts sliding. Two soldiers approached and grabbed Rani.

Rani shook free and glared at them. "You're supposed to work for me. You know Momma's lost it."

"Just come," one of them said.

Maggie shrugged. "Later."

The soldiers escorted Rani down the hall back to Momma Cat. Rani eyed the Persian who had whispered in her ear earlier.

The Persian soldier continued to look ahead. They arrived at the yellow arched entry and the two tall black gate sentries swung open the creaking double doors.

"Sobered up?" Momma whined.

"Huh?"

Momma leaned to breathe in her face and narrowed her eyes to slits. "Have you removed any thoughts of escaping your loving Mom?"

"Of course." Rani gulped.

"Bring him," Momma said, flicking her nails.

A guard dragged a Johok before her and threw him to the polished stone floor. "This little rat humper told me a very interesting story."

"Oi's was jus' sayin'–"

"Quiet!" Momma snapped. "Rancid beast."

"What's this about?" Rani demanded. She growled at the Johok and eyed them both carefully.

"Our little friend here brought home a present for you."

"What… present?"

"An X1 supercharged hybrid tabby turbo tiger Interceptor."

Rani gulped again. "Manx?"

Momma smiled. "Ahh, so you know the driver?"

Rani flicked her blonde rag hair off her face and forced a smile. "Driver? Hah! That's me."

Momma nodded. "Very good. And… anything else? Hmm?"

Rani shook her head.

"I see, dear child." Momma growled at the Johok. "Well this low life mentioned a TomTom but we searched the car and it's not there."

"Where is it?" Momma screeched to the Johok.

"Sorry ma'am, I… I–"

"To the Tray with you; go join that other useless Johok. Maybe you can jog each other's mem'ry."

Momma motioned to the guards and they dragged the struggling Johok away.

"Now, dear, I have sent some of your loving, loyal soldier friends to keep watch over our new vehicle, as the other Johoks can't be trusted. Who knows what we may find when we search it?"

Rani nodded slowly and forced another smile.

"Go back to Maggie," she said, ushering. "You are both free to wander. Just don't get any more ideas… until I am ready."

Rani swung back to eye Momma carefully. "Ready?"

"Shoo."

Rani flung out her arm and open paw to the approaching escort who stepped back.

Rani bit her lip as the doors closed behind her. What a stupid day, she thought.

7: Pride Mountain

The sun reached low past the horizon, the yellow light outlining bike and tabby as he rode up the ravine. The mountain loomed over him in the dusk and he pulled up to the side of the ravine near a narrow cave.

A scorpion clambered over a rock and he stared at it for a moment. He dismounted and wheeled the Yamaha into a craggy section of rock. Rocks clattered nearby. He looked up and eyed the ravine carefully for any hint of a felid shape around the cliff outlines in the low light. He caught a glimpse between two sharp reaches of rock of the larger ravine beyond.

He probed his leather jacket and then cursed. He fell back against a rock and gripped his head tight, realizing he did not have the locator.

"What's chef got cookin' tonight?" A gravelly voice spoke nearby.

Manx crouched back into the shadows.

"Satay goanna, again. That gib cook's always on with the goanna. Probably got knackered by one."

The voices laughed; the sound bouncing down the cave walls.

"Puke to goanna I say. I wan' more eel from the underground basin," said the other voice.

Manx stepped through the narrow rocky mouth where it tapered away into a fissure, and he inched himself sideways down the angled crevice wall to get a look. He heard the sound of machines, spark welders, and grinding. Some cats were singing. He spotted a large cavern filled with tom and catgirl mechanics, working on semis, buggies, and bikes. He spotted the Interceptor under an arcing spray of sparks; the vehicle parked next to a two-person Quadratwirl, a quad rotor gyrocopter, he mused, the blades folded up.

He spotted five welders singing as they worked…

"Everything is stupid,

"Every single part doesn't go with the rest

"Everything is stupid but we pound it to fit

"Just like a Feral face pushed in the shit

"Everything is stupid,

"We're building motors but we run out of juice

"And bigger trailers that get stuck on the roof

"Everything is stupid…"

Someone blew a horn and the workers downed tools and trudged out of the cavern.

Manx poked his head through the crevice as a cold breeze rushed in behind him. He stepped down a shallow slope of rocks and kept low, working his way to the Interceptor.

He looked up and about, scoping the area for any strays and then lifted the trunk of his vehicle. He probed under some rubbish someone had left, felt shards of broken glass and reached for a latch.

He lifted a panel and removed his crossbow and arrows, slotting the arrows in his shoulder guard, and one into the mini crossbow which clicked onto a bracket belt on the arm of his jacket. He grabbed a small jar from the hidden compartment and pocketed it. He peered over to the back seat, and then snuck about to ease the door open. He probed the under dash compartment and then stretched his arm under the seats and felt across the diamond plate floor.

Manx cursed under breath, "Shit, where is it?"

Two cats laughed in the distance and Manx crouched low and eased out of the vehicle. Then he heard someone cough and looked about. He observed how much dust was on his car and thought the Johok must have had some fun in the desert. He began to wipe the glass and then stopped, using his toe-finger to write on the windshield, *'fix rear nitro tank and refill –Momma'*.

He turned for the crevice when two toms lunged out of the shadows and grabbed him.

"We's gotcha," one large rancid tom breathed into his face, his yellow eyes bloodshot as he held Manx down.

The other pushed on his chest. "Noice six pack, not loike a Feral. One of Momma's humpers?" He wheezed and then coughed hard. "Cockflincher's gonna be rool pleased with this taut bloke."

"Yews mean tortoise shell?"

"Frick off idiot," hissed the other tom. "He's a tabby with no tail." He broke into a laugh.

Manx swung his fist into the tom's flapping jaw and felt the mushy skin sink back into nothing. He swung at the other and rolled over onto his back on the dusty floor, before lifting his arm up and releasing an arrow.

The arrow flew into the other tom's eye and he screamed, staggering backwards, falling against the truck.

Manx got up and ran towards the crevice when he saw catgirl soldiers approaching; the same ones he had seen with Rani. He produced the small jar from his pocket, flicked the lid back and hurriedly dipped the arrowheads in it as he ran under cover behind a semi-trailer.

The catgirl fired a bullet that just missed his leg.

Manx loaded an arrow, pulled the frame back and released.

It hit her shoulder. She staggered, dropping her gun before falling.

The other tom tripped over her as he lunged for Manx who shot another arrow.

Manx spotted a tunnel behind the vehicles and ran. Bullets pinged off the pipes above him as he raced up the roughly hewn winding tunnel, thinking he was going up into the mountain. He spotted a rusted section of tubing and fired another arrow as he passed it. The pipe exploded and tore away; dropping to burst a jet of steam.

The other soldiers fell back, covering their eyes.

Manx ran further into the tunnels and came to a fork. He hesitated and took the right-hand one which went lower for a time, and then sharply upwards. He reached an opening and realized he was on a balcony surround by sculptured marble teeth and fangs with flaming torches strapped to them. He leaned over the toothy edge as the cool breeze chilled the sweat on his face. He looked down to see hundreds of cats gathered below, some stoking fires, others singing, and another being whipped. He gasped and swung about to face the torches on the walls behind him, billowing and woofing with the breeze.

The shadow of someone stretched across the wall of the tunnel beyond that he just came from. It wavered and changed shape but came no further.

Something creaked above his head. A catgirl straddling a metal chain, one paw swinging on a loading hook, kicked him in the head with her steel-capped boot.

Manx fell over, face in the ground.

"Not again," He grumbled, before passing out.

8: The Tray

"Where's the other?"

Manx felt the grip around his neck as he lay on the marble floor. He flung his eyes open to see Rani sitting on him, pinning both his arms to the floor; she glared and hissed, her rag hair dropping over his face, tickling his whiskers.

Manx grinned. "I hardly know you."

She squeezed tighter. "*Where* is the other? Did he go to the cat's mouth with you?"

Manx tried to shrug his shoulders under her pressing arms; he smiled awkwardly.

Rani looked down to his crotch pressed against hers. "Are you pitching?"

"Nuh-uh," Manx said flatly before smiling.

Manx spotted Maggie standing behind her, paws on hips, and then he noticed a rotund ginger sprawled across a massive cushion. A squat, short-legged punkhawallah servant cat stood next to her, fanning her bulbous face.

Rani hissed. "Tell me where the other one is!"

"It's Simmons, Rani," Maggie said.

Manx spluttered, "Dead."

"Boolsheeit," Rani said, glaring at him. "He's skulking about in this citadel."

"Johok got'im, back in the desert." Manx choked on his words.

Rani released her grip and crouched over him. She turned to Momma. "I believe him." She sighed. "But he killed some of my… our soldiers. They're dead too, thanks to this bastard."

Manx looked at her, his face turning white.

Maggie shook her head slowly, a tear emerging from her eye. "Simmons was lovely."

"You didn't know him," she blurted at Maggie. She turned to Manx. "And we don't know you."

"Ask him for it," Momma wheezed. She flicked the back of her paw at her fanning servant and said, "Enough, Ball-less. Leave."

Rani glared at Manx. "Where is it?"

Manx screwed his face.

"The TomTom, you stupid road tiger."

"Not with me."

"Duh," Maggie said.

"Not with X1?" Manx asked.

"So you stashed it somewhere here then?" Momma said, her green eyes opening wide. She pulled on the flex tube and yelled into the cone, "Gonad… Gonad!"

"Yes ma'am?" replied the scratchy voice.

"Ask Major Tom to order a search for a camera GPS spotter. It's a TomTom, early 2018 16K resolution model that links to the satellite above that has the 20k terrain sensor."

"Yes ma'am."

Rani eyed her oddly.

Manx sat up, scratching his head. "No wonder it sucks the batteries," he grumbled.

"You think I'm an idiot?" Momma glared at him. "I know what it is. I know you took it from Immodium Jack, because he took it from me. And now I'll find it here in my own mountain." She waved to the soldiers standing nearby. "We don't need him, we can find it ourselves. Take him to the Tray."

Manx fell back onto the paws of the two soldiers who heaved him upright.

Manx blinked hard. The room swayed as he tried to stand; and as they swung him about to the main yellow arched doors he suddenly laughed.

"What's wrong with him, Maggie?"

"Dunno, Rani. He's mad. Gotta be."

Manx pointed to the doors and cackled. "Golden arches... a Micky Dees Maccas entrance. Very chic, Momma."

Momma rolled her big green eyes. "The Tray'll wake him up. Then he'll talk some sense."

- - -

Leather-clad guards wearing metal grilled helmets with holes where the ears poked through dragged Manx down the tunnels, his paws behind his back, wrapped in chains. He wondered why the metalworkers didn't weld ear protectors for the guards but guessed they needed to hear orders.

As they went deeper down into the mountain Manx noticed how the walls appeared wet, the pipes glistening above them, probably from condensation. The soil was soft underneath, almost mushy. He heard screams and cries in the distance which grew louder as they approached.

They walked past another tunnel, more brightly lit by bulbs haphazardly thrown together along a ceiling conduit. He spotted a sign on the wall that said 'Generators and Methane Plant'.

They walked further for a time and then entered a large chasm. Stalactites hung from the ceiling which tapered to a point high above the center of the chasm. A circle of balconies jutted from the rock face further down. Manx looked forward to see many cages the size of two road trains side-by-side and scattered about, surrounded by channels of streaming water.

He coughed. A pungent smell rasped up his nostrils.

A burly tom stood at a cage door. He was completely covered in leather, and metal wheel hubs for chest plates, and baring leather straps covered in wheel nuts.

The tom reached for the giant key ring on his belt. He opened the creaking steel door and sneered. "Welcome to the Tray. You're sure gonna love it here."

Manx looked quizzically at the skinny Persian soldier beside him and asked, "Why's this called The Tray?"

She laughed. "Haven't figured yet?"

The burly tom pushed him into the giant cage and he fell to the soft ground, a mix of sand and gritty salt which burned the sores on his knuckles.

And then he spotted the Johoks. He rolled on his side, thrusting his legs back through the chain loop. He got up and lunged at them, swinging his chain-bound wrists.

A prod dug into his back and sparked.

Manx juddered and fell over.

The Johoks stepped back as the burly tom prodded Manx again. "None of that in 'ere. Momma needs y'all in one piece." He held up the prod and it sparked. He pointed to a slider switch on the barrel and said, "That was a low setting."

The two Johoks sat there and stared at the burly tom, eyes wide open. They nodded quickly.

Manx lay on the sand and glared at them, and then huffed. He looked up to see that the cage also had bars across the top; and then he spotted dried flecks of shit splattered across the bars.

Someone released a fart.

Manx looked to the shadows behind him to spot a large aged yellow cat slumped in the corner, orange eyes glowing in the half light, a big grin on its face, it's pair of dirty beige-colored incisors glinting in the light.

"What's your problem?" Manx asked.

The yellow cat sighed. "Fresh. I like fresh. Hope you brought me fresh."

Manx coughed and held his nose as the sharp stench of dung filled his nostrils.

The yellow cat dug his hind legs into the soil and kicked. He then howled, "What a lovely traaaay!"

One of the Johok's laughed. "Now ya know what the Tray is, mate. Don' worry, they rake it every week." He scoffed at the fat yellow cat. "Savin' for later, ay?"

Manx raised one eyebrow and eyed the Johok. "Yellow cat eats…?"

The Johok laughed again. "Don' worry about 'ol Scat Cat. He'll eat anything, but only when it's dead."

"He should eat a couple of dead shits like you two," Manx said.

"Aw, don' be loike that. We can be buddies. I'm Nad, and this scruffy thing is Errol."

"You killed Simmons," Manx said.

"Who? Your pal? You… have a pal?"

Manx smirked.

"Oh it's not us," Nad said, opening his arms out as he smiled. "We's just take cars."

"You took my car."

Errol leaned towards Manx and grinned, bearing bluish yellow teeth. "Seems everybloody wants your car."

"Make way," someone yelled high above them.

"Oh gawd, it's butthole time; here we go agin," Errol said as they all looked up. The two Johoks moved to one side of the cage.

Manx looked up high to see a cat's ass poking over the ledge of one of the balconies. The cat dumped, the dung dropping down to splat on the bars above them, and into the cage, just missing Manx.

Another cat poked it's ass over the ledge of another balcony and released.

Manx and the Johoks ran to the other side of the cage.

"Watchunda!" Another cat high above yelled.

"Shit Nad, this time it's vomit," Errol gasped.

A sepia, green, and orange stream splattered across the cage as the occupants crouched down and hid their faces.

The cage door clanged open and they saw the burly tom standing there.

"Oi, Momma wants ta talk with you, tailless one."

Manx gripped the collar of Nad and growled. "You took my car. Where is the TomTom?"

"TomTom?"

"Where is it," he asked, clenching tighter.

"'Urry up tigerlily," the burly tom screeched at Manx, waving his arm. "Like it in there already do you? All those nice fat g-bombs...I'm not walkin' across *that* to get ya."

"WHERE IS IT?" Manx yelled into Nad's ear.

"I tossed it," Errol said quickly. "Useless thing."

"Where?" Manx demanded.

"Where we left you, at Fur Ridge, you know, 'dems yellow road eaters."

The curl of a whip lashed around Manx's neck and tugged him back. Manx gripped the braided leather and jerked about to see the burly tom guard grinning as he pulled on the long whip. "Here kitty; I also got a cat o' nine tails whip in me back pocket, just for you."

Manx gripped the whip and with one hard tug, pulled the burly tom to trip and fall into the fresh droppings from above.

The guard's voice muffled through the sand and dung, "Oh crap."

"Ooh, fresh," Scat cat hummed. "I like fresh...."

Manx swung to Errol before leaving. "By the way, there's crap on your furhawk." He looked up quickly to see a tom standing on the ledge high above, unbuttoning his fly.

"You need a shower too," Manx said as he darted over the massive guard trying to heave himself up.

The Persian soldier waiting outside took his arm.

Manx looked at her twisted grin and nodded to his arm. "I see you picked the clean side."

"Don't worry," She said, "We'll scrub you up before you see Momma."

Manx glanced back at the guard.

The burly tom spat and waved a fist at him, and yelled, "Next time!" His face was covered in shit.

9: The Sinking Desert

"Feeling fresh now?" Rani asked as she approached him.

Manx looked her slender shape up and down and nodded, and said, "Fresh."

Rani touched his clean leather jacket and pants. "Hmm, I see they gave you a new belt."

"I'd like my crossbow back," he said flatly.

"Not after what you did–"

"I didn't kill them. It was knockout gel."

"I know," Rani said lightly. "I know now. You could be a real handy asset for us."

"Here?" Manx asked as he looked about the plush room filled with mirrors and dressing tables.

"We normally use the Grooming Room for Momma's sires. It could suit you too," she said as she walked past him, lightly trailing her partly retracted claws across his face.

Manx huffed. "Sires."

"Oh don't be so mocking, dear Manxy babe. Fear not; I see you doing something else for us, perhaps working alongside Major Tom."

"Where was he when he wasn't at home?" Manx asked, thinking of her convoy.

"High overhead."

"What?" Manx then nodded slowly.

"Games," Rani said. "Momma plays games. I still don't know why, but I do know she's right."

Manx looked at her oddly. "But before, you said–"

"Shhhhh…" she held her paw to his lip and stroked his whiskers. "Come…" She took his paw gently, her wide steel-blue eyes beaming at him. "Momma will explain."

- - -

Immodium Jack farted.

The tunnel echoed the sound.

The Ferals behind stopped for a moment and then continued. Immodium held his flashlight and aimed it down the tunnel, the steel tracks running into flickering water.

"These tunnels'll soon be useless," Tailbutt said as they sloshed their way down towards the base of the mountain.

"Our inside tom sez it's getting' much worse. And my scout barely got out alive, but then he kept diving for water rats, the stupid fricktard."

Tailbutt shook his scruffy head and blinked, and then ducked as Immodium lifted his leg.

"Hah hah, jus' kiddun," Immodium laughed. "Pity we can't take the loco in; is better parked behind the ridge in Momma's radar blind spot. They jus' better stay until we give the signal at the Tooth Terrace cat's mouth after we kill the generators. They won't have Jock to fix it this time."

"What about our inside boy?" Tailbutt asked.

Immodium rubbed his sodden jaw, his eyes narrowing. "I don' trust 'im. He better disable the gyrocopter first before blowin' the horn. He's not real bright; comes with havin' a biggun."

"Yeah," a shorter Feral uttered under breath.

"Wow, we's really organized," someone else whispered in the shadows, "That don't sound like us."

Tailbutt hissed as the water lapped around his waist. "No wunda Momma abandoned this side of the mountain, it's a bleed'n' lake now."

"Shan't go much deeper," Immodium said. "If so, we's gonna get even wetter. Chroist I hate water."

They waded further down the tunnel and reached a rusted bulkhead door; water lapped up to the flywheel.

"Okay, it's tuggun' time," Tailbutt said.

The Ferals looked at each other and stepped back.

Tailbutt shook his head. "No, not that, you chook-choking idiots."

Immodium Jack flexed his massive soiled arms and paws and gripped the rusty wheel. He jerked it. It budged just an inch. "Not impressed," he huffed.

Tailbutt turned to the Feral gang. "Now who 'ere's strong enuff to turn that wheel?"

"Oi will," muttered a short black and white Feral wearing oversized leathers and a dog's skull bone round his neck.

The others laughed, the hollow sound bouncing down the tunnel.

"Shhhhh…" Tailbutt ushered him to the door.

The short Feral gripped the wheel, and then nodded to his three short friends. They joined him and all four tugged the wheel in the opposite direction. It loosened and then spun freely as they let go.

Immodium farted again. "Smart. Rool smart." He spotted Tailbutt rolling his eyes and he slapped him across the head. "I knows. Was just seeing 'ow smart the rest of you are, heh heh." He gripped the rusted door handle and yanked hard. It opened a couple of inches and water from the tunnel rushed past them.

"Okay me lil' squat Fezzas, come an' 'ave another tug with me."

Immodium Jack gripped the edge of the door as the others pulled at the rusted handle, heaving the door open.

Water rushed past them into the lit tunnel beyond.

Immodium Jack smiled. "We're in!"

- - -

"So here we are again," Momma breathed as she preened her huge paw, her lumpy tongue lashing her ginger fur as she eyed them both. "So... my locator; are you ready to talk?"

Manx grinned. "You didn't find it then, Mommy."

Rani slapped his face.

Manx eyed her sharply. "It's at Fur Ridge."

"What?"

"Blame the Johoks," Manx said flatly.

Momma sat upright, creasing her face with anger. "Excuses! You useless tabby with no tail." She stretched opened her mouth and hissed; all the fur on her back rose and everyone stepped back, except Manx.

"It's not his fault, Momma. We'll find another one," Rani said.

"There's no time," Momma said quietly. "We need to leave here."

Rani tilted her head and looked oddly at her. "But all this time…"

"I know," Momma hissed. "We had to give you an incentive to leave, and go after you and see where you went. We *wanted* you to feel uncomfortable here. This place is sinking. We have less than a year before the generators get flooded."

"But water's good isn't it? We can trade water for fuel. We're running out of fuel."

"No Rani," she said through a sigh, her head drooping. "Your Pop was right. And I mistreated him so."

"What? I thought *he* was the bastard."

"He was right all along," she whined. "This mountain will eventually be an island. The salt table from the Great Artesian is rising. There will be no fresh water. And the roads are being eaten too."

Rani took in a deep breath and Manx eyed her carefully.

"Those creeping crinoids are everywhere," she said.

"Yes my dear daughter. They're hardy, and evolved quickly from all the acid rain and fallout from the Old War. Look at their stupid spiny fronds and those big bulbs. You'd think they get lots o' rain, but nothing. It doesn't rain here, ever. It comes from underneath, and they sure don't need fresh water."

Momma fell back against the cushion and sighed. "And now we may not have enough fuel to leave here."

"You could have saved the fuel instead of using it to chase us," Rani blurted.

"Ma'am..." Manx raised a paw.

Momma glared at him. "I should put you to a duel with Cockflincher, see who's stronger. Then we can then use you for breeding, instead of trying to trade salty water for a skinny northern tom, or stealing a Feral."

"I know where you can get fuel," Manx said.

Rani turned to him and folded her arms. "How?"

Momma hissed at him. "Trying to buy your way out with lies again?"

"Again?" Manx cringed.

The lights flickered.

"I don't trust outsiders, I just rule them," Momma hissed.

The lights shut out, leaving the sun to highlight the swirling dust and their stark faces as the beams angled inside through narrow rocky slits.

An alarm then shrilled above them and Manx and Rani quickly glanced at each other.

Momma's communication funnel screeched and they heard the tiny voice at the other end yell, "Ferals!"

"How many?"

"Can't tell."

She gripped the voice cone. "Use the backup generator for the radar and keep the comms charged, and pray it don't die 'cos Jock's not here to fix it." Momma spoke louder into the tube, "Soldiers and guards to the lower levels; ready our convoy. It's time to leave."

Major Tom strode into the hall and saluted Momma.

Manx eyed this strange black and white spotted cat, dressed in an Old War uniform, green khaki, and wearing jackboots and carrying a cane. Oversized pilot goggles sat atop his head, his fluffed-up spotted ears stopping them from slipping off.

"I say, this must be an attack, Queen Mom. I'll ride the quadcopter and reconnoiter the Black Ridge."

"Go, Major," ordered Momma.

Major Tom saluted and left.

"The Ferals will be using the old mining track," Momma said quickly, "to the back of this mountain. But the tunnels are flooded, there can't be too many of those catrats coming in from there. The Major will fly around Black Ridge, where they'll no doubt be hiding Thunderball, their stupid skull-mounted loco and cadre of vehicles. Our radar doesn't ping there, too much iron in the rocks."

Maggie ran into the hall, wearing thick gloves and carrying a steel boomerang. "I'm ready to fight those catrats," she said aloud.

"You gotta be kidding me," Manx said flatly.

Rani grinned. "She's good!"

"Take your Intratec too," Momma said.

Maggie nodded fast and grinned.

"Sheesh," Manx breathed.

"And what will *you* do Little No-tail? This isn't your war."

Manx looked her square in the eye... and said nothing.

"I thought so," Momma said, folding her big ginger arms. "Go back to that desert you love so much. Just remember, it will be a bog pit one day. The future belongs to the mud."

"We don't need you," Maggie blurted.

Manx turned and brushed Rani's shoulder. "I want my weapons," he said flatly.

"In your car, asshole."

Manx walked out alone, the golden arched doors creaking shut behind him.

Rani kept staring at the closed doors, which opened again as some guards approached. She shook her head.

Manx made his way down the tunnels as soldiers rushed past him towards the generator rooms. He spotted a shadow moving down a side tunnel and he slowed.

A steel-capped fist lunged out, just nicking his chin. Manx fell back against the rocky wall.

A large, dirty-white tom wearing a brake cable harness stood over him, adjusting himself. "So, you's the one causing all the trouble, ay? Knew I'd seen you's before."

Manx eyed him carefully. "Who the frick are you?"

"Momma wanted you to replace me," the large cat said. "I'm Cockflincher, and I'm *better* than you."

"Sure, whatever you say, Cockfarter," Manx said, dusting himself off as he stood up.

"I *hate* my name bein' twisted. You's gonna pay. You were meant to duel me," Cockflincher breathed. "And Momma was gonna reward me with more pussies."

Two guards brushed past, racing down the tunnels, seemingly ignoring them.

"But Momma betrayed me," Cockflincher continued. "So I lets the Ferals in."

"What?" Manx cringed.

"Now…" Cockflincher patted the big metal-clad cow horn on his belt, "… I'm gonna tell the rest 'o 'em Ferals to come."

"You–"

"Dat's roight," Cockflincher swung his fist. "I no's longer work for Momma. I's work for Immodium Jack."

Manx ducked, and swung a left into the tom's groin.

Cockflincher keeled over and Manx threw a right punch across his jaw, knocking him face down to the ground. "That's for spoiling my left fist," he said. He shook his paws to loosen the fingers. He wiped the back of his left paw across the back of Cockflincher's knotted rat jacket. He removed the horn from the big cat's belt, placed it on the stony ground, and stomped his boot down on it.

Manx turned and headed for the vehicle chamber as more guards raced past him. He entered the chamber and saw a massive, distant wall on the other side judder, silt flaking off it. It groaned and shifted, tilting back and upwards to the ceiling on immense iron pivots. The sun raced into the darkness, highlighting the dusty outlines of the various vehicles.

"The blasted gyro won't engage," Major Tom said as he spat on the ground. He unclipped his harness and placed it on the hood of the Interceptor.

"Watch my car," Manx said as he approached the odd-looking quadcopter and pilot.

"I don't suppose you know about electric motive force, do you?" asked Major Tom.

Manx looked at him quizzically. "British?"

"By Jove you have a quick mind," Major Tom replied with a chuckle.

"My friend was British. Now he's dead," Manx said flatly.

"Your car's there asshole," someone spoke as he ran past Manx.

"Don't worry about Spanky," the Major said. "I'm sorry to hear this."

Manx examined the battery pack, strung by rope to the underside of the two-person machine. "Hmm… Lithium polymers."

"Yes," the Major said. "These are the stable, high capacity ones. Can go three hundred miles on one charge." He pointed to the underside. "More batteries in those other compartments below."

Manx scratched through his whiskers. "Impressive."

"Lucky I charged this beast, since the mountain's power is down to auxiliary. Help me wheel it outside, through that Thunderbird Two hangar door. Momma's depending on us."

Manx cringed at him, and then dragged the gyrocopter with the Major pushing; he noticed one of the wheels had a flat.

"Those blasted yellow plants," The Major said.

Manx opened another battery compartment door. "Look," he said, pointing, "Someone's removed a busbar."

Major Tom examined the connections, the metal joiner bar removed from the top of two of the batteries. "Blast, 'ol boy. Detest batteries wired in series." He breathed hard and stood up. "But have no fear, just happen to have some spares in my tool box."

"That fuel tanker trailer," Manx said. "Is she empty?"

"Of course," the Major said. "We're running out of fuel more than we can make it."

Manx eyed the other semi-trailers in the cavern. "What about those tanks?" he asked, pointing to the many bulbous cylinder shapes under the semi-trailers.

"Not for fuel," Major Tom said. "They have air compressors; I hope we never have to use them."

"What?"

"Never mind," said the Major. "What do you want the fuel tanker-trailer for? You'll need a prime mover."

"Got one?" Manx asked, "And gas to drive her?"

"Ahem, think so. But w–"

Manx took off for the tanker, grabbing Spanky by the scruff of his neck and dragging him away from underneath the Interceptor.

"Hey, me shoulder still hurts!"

"Boohoohoo."

"Yours would too if you had to jump off a flipping semi," Spanky wheezed.

"Nobody touches my car."

"Just looking," Spanky said. "And see, I replaced your spare nitro tank, and filled it, just like Momma asked."

Manx smirked.

"That hybrid wheel system is awesome. You design it?"

"Yes," Manx said as he looked beyond the open rocky hangar door.

"They's say you're leaving here, you won't help Momma."

"You're coming with me," Manx said flatly. "With *that*." He pointed.

"The tanker? Empty. Ya can't steal vapor."

"I want it empty. Hook up the tractor unit and make sure the gas tank is full. And get me some hoses, clamps, and as many garden shears and clippers as you can find."

Spanky laughed. "Doing some gardening? Why not those Finnish bayonets over there on the rack," he said, pointing.

Manx eyed the scruffy big yellow-eyed black cat in greasy overalls and smirked again. He then shrugged his shoulders.

Spanky nodded and grinned stupidly.

"And you're coming with me," Manx said.

"Aw jeez, I like going out. That trip chasin' Rani was fun. Uses fuel though. Bet Cockflincher will be jealous."

Manx shook his head. "C'mon, scruffbones. You're driving."

1D: Fight or Run

"Caught a dozen Ferals in the generator room, and two near the Tray," the silver cat guard said. "They were heading back to the sunken bulkhead; we not seen the big ugly dirty-white one but we'll find him soon."

"Hmm..." Momma pawed under her chin as she purred to herself. "Keep looking, in case Immodium hasn't scurried back to his sodden pals. He may be skulking around the kitchen area; he has a bad habit of eating and farting, often at once. I don't want food spoils. We need to take what we can."

"Yes ma'am."

"Now what about other preparations to leave?"

"Generators are taking longer than expected–"

Momma rolled her eyes and sighed. "If only I hadn't sent that Scottish Fold away. Forget the generators."

"The vehicles are primed, but..." the silver guard's face turned white.

"But what?"

"Gas tanker three has been taken."

Momma sat up and grimaced.

"The Interceptor is still here," the guard continued. "Rani says she'll drive it."

"Will she now?" Momma tapped her lips and then hissed. "What's he up to, taking a tanker?"

"It's empty. The others are full now," the guard said. "That's our last tiger methane."

Momma opened her eyes wide and tapped her lips again. "He's either an idiot, or..." She flicked the back of her paw at another guard. "The Heathkit."

The guard ran to the side of the chamber and opened a pair of old wooden doors, returning with a rusted metal case. He unclipped the lid to reveal a panel of dials and a microphone; he clipped a battery to it and ran a cable from the control panel to a big round wall socket.

Momma picked up the microphone. "Major Tom, this is ground control. You copy?"

"Adjust the VSWR," the guard said.

"Yes, yes." Momma turned a dial until a soft yellow light glowed across the instrument panel. "Major Tom, this is ground control."

A voice crackled back, "Here Commander, over Black Ridge."

Momma sneered at the Burmese guard standing nearby. "I wish he'd stick to the same title."

The guard giggled.

"Momma wants a status report," she said softly.

The speaker crackled.

"Major Tom!"

"Major Tom to ground control... Planet Earth is red and everything is dead."

Momma cringed. "Report on the Ferals at once!" she snapped.

"They're still at Black Ridge, not doing anything, just... sitting there. But occasionally–"

The sound of a bullet shrilled and crackled through the speaker.

"–they take pot shots at me."

"Keep your distance. What are they waiting for? A signal?" Momma looked to the nearest guard. "Go bring one of the Ferals to me."

The guard nodded and left the chamber.

Momma clicked the microphone. "Major... Land near a high spot and double back to keep an eye on the Feral road trains. And be ready for when we leave. I'll get the girls to fire up the drones once we leave the mountain's shadow. I want to find that tailless wanker."

"By your jolly command, General!" Major Tom said confidently.

Momma shook her head.

The guard returned, dragging a hissing black and gray Feral into the chamber. The cat swung about, claws extended, swishing the air with every throw of the paw.

"Hold him down," Momma ordered.

She approached the Feral as she flicked her tail about. She glared at the shabby cat before her. As the others held the Feral down, Momma stomped her boot down on its tail.

The Feral screamed and squirmed.

Momma breathed on the creature and bared all her incisors. "Where's Immodium Jack?"

Tailbutt squirmed. "Dunno, but you'd know if he was coming by the smell," he said as he twitched his nose.

"Don't be impudent little Feral," Momma scoffed. "I know you're Tailbutt, Immodium Jack's right-hand Feral."

"Sometimes left hand," Tailbutt chuckled, "depends which side he drops one."

Momma pressed her boot onto Tailbutt's neck. "Why're you here? Where are the rest of them?"

"We…" Tailbutt coughed and gripped her boot. "… let go!"

Momma eased off.

"The horn," Tailbutt spluttered. "We di'n' hear it. But Immodium insisted we still go inside, see? All the other Ferals sloshed back down the tunnel."

Momma sighed and released her boot. "I know why you're here. You want the TomTom." She breathed hard into his face. "Well we don't have it. That stub-tail Manx does. And now he's gone."

Tailbutt sat up, his face pallid.

"Enough!" Momma clicked her claws. "Take him back to the Tray, and then inspect the kitchen. I bet you Immodium will be there by now, stuffing his puffy white face under that stupid dogtooth muzzle of his."

The guards heaved up Tailbutt and dragged him away, just as two soldiers returned.

"Well?" Momma folded her arms.

"Got away, Commissar," the tall Russian Blue gasped. "Heard shitting sound in corridor and inwistigitid the kitchin. Kitchin stunk. We caught him takin' dump into a wigetable pan, while cussing someone called Flincher."

Momma stood upright and stomped her boot on the marble floor. "So...you have him?"

"Nyet, Commissar, I winted to sleet his thloat but he dlopped a giant splishing grivity bomb. We could barely breathe!"

"Cowards," Momma hissed. "Keep looking or *you* will wind up in the Tray!"

The soldiers bowed and turned for the door.

"And get pegs for your noses!" Momma yelled after them.

Momma hissed again. "*Flincher...* Where the hell is Cockflincher?"

One guard shrugged.

The other guard said, "I heard of a dust up with that tailless cat, near the vehicle chamber."

"Why didn't you..." She gripped the tube inlet cone and yelled into it, "Spanky... Bring me Cockflincher!"

A chilly air gushed out through the hose, causing her whiskers to retract.

"Rani! Anyone!"

Nobody replied.

Momma turned to her Persian guard. "They must be readying the vehicles outside. I am guessing Immodium Jack's probably retreated down the tunnels and back to his convoy. That means his road train may knock down our front door next. We don't have enough fuel to engage–"

"Let alone cross the desert," the guard interjected.

"I *know*," Momma snapped at her. "We must go now. But get some boys up here to quickly clear my stuff, and make sure my rig is ready to leave –and don't forget my telly."

- - -

"They'll catch up with us," Spanky said.

"Quiet. Keep driving. We'll be stopping at Fur Ridge."

"Why there? It's horrible; the plants have come onto the road, they're eating it."

"Something I need," Manx said. "And something you need."

"They should have taken the alternate route, less plants," Spanky said.

"You know about that?"

"Everyone knows about it," Spanky said with surprise in his eyes. "Going this way, they'll be on our tail soon," he said nervously.

"Who? The Ferals? Or Momma?"

Spanky looked to the horizon and ignored Manx.

Manx then noticed Spanky had no tail. "What the frick?"

Spanky glanced down. "You'se looking at my ass, dipshit?"

"You got no tail."

"So?"

"Neither have I, if you haven't noticed."

Spanky coughed. "Yeah, when I was a kitten," he said slowly, "they came to our village. This one guy; tall and ugly puma-like thing with a huge black furhawk. He was taking tails."

"Tailcutter," Manx said quietly. He glared at Spanky. "At least they don't call you Manx."

Spanky sighed. "That was a long time ago. I sit better without a tail. Don't you?"

Manx grunted and fiddled about with his sawed-off.

Somebody sniggered.

"What's so funny?" Manx asked Spanky.

"I didn't say anything."

Manx looked about the cabin of the tractor unit and noticed the sleeping compartment was closed.

"Almost at Fur Ridge," Spanky said.

Holding his gun, Manx slowly got up and flung the hatch open.

A Johok fell onto the back seat. Manx thrust his arm into the compartment and pulled out another Johok.

"Jeez!"

"Shutup Spanky, keep driving."

Manx flicked his gun to the pair of them and shook his head. "You two," he grumbled.

"We wan' no trubble," Nad said, holding out open paws.

"No, no twubble," Errol said.

"Hand over your guns, knives, whatever."

"Got none since the Tray," Errol said. "That big cat with the prong tried to zap *us* for what *you* did to 'im. I insulated me paws in dry dung and pulled on his prod–"

"You mean we's did," Nad said.

"Yeah, we's both pulled the guy and he fell face first in the fresh shit again."

Manx offered a half smile and then huffed. "Now that you're here, you'll be useful."

The pair of Johoks looked at each oddly.

"Why Manx?" asked Spanky.

"More hands for gardening," he said flatly. With sawed-off pointing to Nad, Manx threw a left punch across Errol's jaw.

"Wha's that for?" Errol squealed.

Nad sat up.

Manx raised his gun.

"For knocking me out and taking my car," Manx said.

"But... but that was Nad!" Errol said and thumbed to Nad.

Manx said flatly, "He's still got shit on his face. You don't."

- - -

Momma watched the girls in the Interceptor howl with glee as they revved the car and made circles in the dust. She ushered her carriers to stop. She stood awkwardly under the hangar door and stumbled over some pebbles.

Rani watched her approach and winced.

"Stop this now. It's not a game this time," Momma boomed, her voice carrying across the canyon.

"You sure?" Maggie asked.

Momma waved her clenched fist. "If I were any smaller I'd be in that car with you. She turned to the soldiers. "Where's my RV? And sort those toms," she said, pointing to the cattle-haulers.

"They should be free," Rani blurted.

"All men are rubbish," Momma said. "They caused the Great Downfall. But be assured, they are working for our *future* –and I don't mean rutting."

Rani scrunched her face at her.

An engine grunted behind them, Momma's iron-clad, part open-top RV rumbling as it drove out from the rocky hangar door.

Momma was helped into the vehicle and sat upon a plush red velvet chair. Bikes were driven into the hold below and Momma sat up, watching a bike approach from around the ridge. "Who's bike is that?"

"Johok Yamahahahaha," the rider said, laughing. "It's filthy." The rider dismounted and removed his plastic helmet, his fluffy tawny ears popping up. He flicked out a knife and cut loose the jerry can strapped to the back.

"Bring that," Momma said, flicking her paws.

The rider handed her the can and she noticed the duct tape. "Clever. This isn't ours, or theirs." She popped the lid, sniffed and coughed. She grabbed a megaphone and yelled to the assembling convoy, "Let's go!"

Momma sat back on her couch as the engines revved and she spotted the Interceptor at the head of the convoy. She held a CB mike and clicked it. "Daughters, dears, you be good kitties and scout ahead."

"This better not be another game," Rani hissed.

Momma sighed. "Where's the Heathkit?"

"Here ma'am," her assistant said.

"Why can't everything be on the same frequency? Forget that; stupid question." She clicked the microphone. "Major Tom, this is ground control."

"They haven't moved," the Major replied.

"Good," Momma breathed. "Then take off; take the lead here and keep an eye on my daughters. They are in the Interceptor."

"Aye-aye... boss."

Momma smiled and aimed the remote to the television mounted on steel posts high above, the screen surround by speakers.

The screen flicked on to show a stage and an orange-eyed British shorthair host wearing a tuxedo, with five Persian beauties dressed in black velveteen evening dresses twerking behind him.

The host adjusted his bow tie. "And now, here's the Spayer Sisters with their number one hit of 2019, 'If only I had a spare Paw to Love You More'."

"I wanted you close but our legs they keep kicking,

"I wanted you close but could not stop licking,

"I wanted you close but the fleas keep itching,

"This life of a cat must be more than just mousing around...

"So...,

"If I only had a spare paw for you...

"If I only had a paw that would do what I tell it to,

"If I only had a spare paw to love you,

"To stroke you while my others parts instinctively go wild..."

The sound of the quadcopter droned overhead.

As the convoy rolled down the hill, Momma looked back to the mountain, to the gaping cat's mouth balcony. She hissed, her tail puffing out as her assistant ducked. "Paw times are upon us. And I'll miss those golden arches."

- - -

"So many plants," Spanky gasped as he smashed the large bulb with a rock, watching the juice squirt from the bottom of the bulb through the open hatch of the trailer tanker. "You sure this works? It could solve all our fuel supply problems,"

"It works," Manx said as he dusted his hands. He pulled out his monocular and aimed it back to Pride Mountain. A hint of dust wafted beyond the horizon. "They'll be here soon."

"Who?" asked Errol, "Momma or da Ferals?"

"Why do you care?"

"I hate dem's both. They treat us like neuters," Nad said.

"Are you?" Manx asked, raising his eyebrows. "Keep smashing those bulbs into the tanker."

"Why're you helping us?" Spanky asked.

"You want to get across the desert? All of you? This is the only way. You'll run out otherwise, and be stuck, and there are worse things ahead of us than you can imagine, much worse than dingoes. Stay in one place and they get you in the night."

Spanky gulped and glanced at the two Johoks who were standing there listening. One dropped a rock.

"Keep moving. We're almost topped up."

"You're the boss," Spanky said, "until Momma gets here."

Manx glared at the black cat and walked off the side of the road.

"Now where are you going?"

"There's a TomTom out here," Manx yelled. "Right, Nad?"

"Bit to the left," Nad said, pointing. "Little more, yeah two steps and you got it."

Manx picked up the locator and dusted it off. He pressed the power button but the screen remained black.

"Why you want that piece of shit?" Nad asked.

"That's the locator Momma talked about," Spanky said. "I know about these. Wow, Manx, that's da model with high resolution satellite feed."

"Need a satellite and high ground," Manx said, "Too much static down here. Too much salt and iron. And we need power. I got solar fabric in the Interceptor." Manx then gripped his face and kicked the tanker tire. "Which I bloody forgot to take."

"No problem," Spanky said, "*our* convoy will get here first."

"Yeah, no one's gonna leave an Interceptor behind," Errol said, laughing.

"I know," Manx said quietly. "Just hope it didn't get cleaned out."

"That was my job," Spanky said. "Shool be roight, moite."

Manx shook his head. He scoped the horizon. The dust haze was bigger.

"You're a bit of a loner, aren't you," Spanky said.

Manx ignored him.

"I know you types," Errol grumbled. "You hate society. Everything bad happens in society."

"Is that what you people have?" Manx asked with a mocking hint in his orange eyes. He held out his arms. "All this...*shit*...is a result of society."

Nad clanked shut the rusted tanker hatch. "All done, boss. What now?"

Manx fixed his eyes on the horizon. "We wait."

11: The Road Loco

Immodium Jack stared out the windshield past the giant iron skull mounted on the pilot wedge. He turned a flywheel as the speakers above played out the tune by Johny Catz...

I fell into a burnin' ring of fire...,

I went down, down, down,

And the fumes went higher,

And it burns, burns, burns,

The ring of fire, a strange desire...

Immodium slapped Cockflincher on the back and grinned through the crooked yellow muzzle teeth. "You're my new right-hand cock."

"Thanks boss. Pity about Tailbutt," Cockflincher said.

Immodium Jack screeched into a microphone as he farted, "Don't let 'em get away from us."

He flicked a couple of switches on the accessory dash in the modified prime mover, a hybrid steam-cooled gas locomotive engine, supported by six triple-coin titan mining truck tires on each side, the stacked wheels mounted on side-coupled connecting rods.

"But keep your distance. Momma will lead us roight to the TomTom and that bastard No-tail."

"What about Tailbutt?" Cockflincher asked, waving his open paw.

Immodium gripped Cockflincher's neck and narrowed his dark eyes. "You wavin' that paw because of the smokebox... or me?"

"Sorry boss, smokebox of course."

Immodium farted again. "The other Ferals will break that scrag out and catch up, and bring supplies," Immodium breathed. "Our priority is Momma's rag tag fleet of homeless kitties on the run, and we need that priceless locator. The Golden City is out there. I can feel it."

"It's all that tailless cat's fault," Cockflincher said. "Thought I remembered him, back when I was a scruffy kitty. My protector handed me nice trophies back in the days of World Die. His was one of them."

"Tailcutter," Immodium Jack said. "My own Feral Pop knew him well.

"Really? Tell me."

"Later," Immodium said, waving his arm as another fart gurgled out. "That would be a long *tail* – especially if you string them all together!" He broke into laughter, farting with every guffaw.

The quadcopter buzzed across the ridge as Immodium waved his studded leather-clad paw for the convoy to head out of the shadows.

Immodium Jack slipped a brass telescope ring over his finger and lifted his paw to the sky, drawing back the smaller glass ring from the larger magnifying disc as he looked through it. "That stupid pilot is angling towards Fur Ridge."

"Glad we didn't knock him off his seat then," Cockflincher said and he clapped his paws. "When's we catch up with Momma, I can finish me business with the tailless one."

"The plants will slow 'em down." He growled down a speaking tube, "Engine room... more power!"

"The tender is full, lad. Ye cannae change the lorse of phissics," came the hollow reply.

"Listen carefully, Jock," Immodium said, hissing into the tube, "you little gray fluff ball... if you don't increase power, I'll slice off those stupid coward ears completely."

"Weel I can try pee'n in the smokebox; it'll ignite a beauty, an' add extra power'," Jock replied, "If that wee helps; had a shot of pure Cat's Piss Whiskey las' night so that aught ta work just fine!"

"That Scottish Fold has a bad attitude," Cockflincher said.

"I heard that, ya Cockflinger!" Jock said through the tube.

Cockflincher slammed the control board. "Asshole! Go shove your sporran down your pants."

"Calls himself a Feral." Immodium grumbled. "Only because Momma dissed him. But we's need smarts. We needs fixers. This engine he modified. We must respect our furgineers. Not like Momma; our gain, her loss." He took the tube. "More power, you muckle fur ball!"

Immodium swung to Cockflincher and breathed heavily through his dogtooth skull muzzle. "We'll take the Rani's secret path to the main road."

Cockflincher raised his eyebrows. "Shit boss, everyone knows that route."

Immodium laughed. "Less ground eaters there, they only like level ground and asphalt; the desert floor is now invaded by these weeds. That alternate route will save us time, and tires."

Immodium Jack pulled the steam whistle.

The Feral convoy mix of converted trains, fuel-tankers and Johok bikes kicked up the red dust as they made their way around the mountain.

- - -

"That cloud's getting bigger," Spanky said. He held up the monocular. "I's can see'em. Big RV with a telly on top and a fat ginger cat with a swishing fan, or is that a tail? And something much closer... your X1."

"Good," Manx said. "They'll need fuel. And I need the solar Stetson."

They watched the approaching Interceptor side-wind around the creeping plants, ducking off the road onto the desert floor, skidding around more plants before jumping back onto the road to slide in a semi-arc, stopping just before them.

Manx looked to Rani and smiled. "Having fun?"

Rani flung open the door and rushed to him, swinging her fist at his face.

Manx ducked and gripped her other arm. "Calm." He breathed heavily and gripped shoulders, looking squarely into her wild blue eyes. "Stop struggling. You're strong. Save your energy."

Rani jerked herself free, flicking back her rag hair. "What the frick are you doing? Why do you care?"

"Thought you'd be long gone by now, pussy," Maggie said to Manx as she got out of the car, Intratec belted to one side, steel serrated boomerang the other.

Spanky jumped down from the tanker, waving both arms high. "Guys, all good; he's helping us."

"By taking an empty fuel tanker?"

"It's full, Rani," Manx said. "Serious."

Rani scrunched her face. "How?"

"Da plants," Errol said, dusting his paws.

Rani and Maggie looked at them incredulously.

"You now have fuel to get you across the desert," Manx said flatly. "Thanks to these bikers."

Nad and Errol grinned.

"If they hadn't knocked me out, taken my car and thrown my TomTom away then I wouldn't have known about the biofuel."

Rani eyed him cautiously. "You're talking too much."

Manx offered a half smile.

"You're liking this!" Rani slapped his side. "You bastard!"

"Well which is it?" Maggie asked.

Rani folded her arms. "But take us to where?"

Manx rummaged through the rear compartment of the Interceptor and produced the solar hat.

"Here comes Momma," Spanky said.

The quad-gyrocopter whizzed overhead and landed on the clear road beyond the plants.

Momma's RV choked and spluttered as it pulled up next to the tanker.

Manx and the others covered their ears as the speakers blared loud the sound of the Back Alley Cats...

"You are on fire,

"My bad desire,

"Believe me when I spray,

"I want it that way–

The sound cut out.

Momma swung about to face Spanky swinging the plug and grinning.

"Yo' bad mofo Spanky," Momma wailed.

"Enough Momma!" Rani screeched. "It's not a game this time and you know it."

Momma pointed to Manx. "Who's the cat in the hat?"

"You want a way across the desert?" Manx asked as he thumbed the TomTom. The screen flickered on; a broken image appeared for a second and then blanked. "We need higher ground than here," he said. "Too much iron in the soil. And I gotta charge this thing."

"Keep yer hat on then." Momma folded her arms as her squat Munchkin cat punkhawalla servant fanned her. She looked to the rising sun. "The hills beyond...that's all I know," she said, "–and The Shells."

"The Shells is a long way from here. But better than going back to Pride Mountain," Spanky said. "I hated those eagles on the mountain top. They crapped something rotten."

"I need fuel," Momma waved to a guard. "Arrange for the rear tanker."

"No need," Manx said. "Nad, get the hose."

Momma sat upright. "You got a Johok to work for you?"

Rani rolled her eyes. "Manx has fuel in this tanker!"

"I know," Momma laughed. "I knew the plants could be useful."

"How?" Rani asked.

"Rinorea asphalifera," Momma said, "The plant that makes my road furry. You can barely drive over it, get spiked if you are unlucky, or just have a darn ugly bumpy ride. It's a mutation, fed by the rising artesian salt water basin underground."

Manx looked away.

"You, tailless one, left a Johok Yamahahaha at the foot of the ravine. The tank was near full. And yet you came all the way from here, no doubt."

"It's high octane," Manx said. "Mixture may be off in an RV; get Spanky to set the fuel mix right, don't let it run rich."

Spanky glared at him. "You giv'un orders again? Thanks, tailless one."

Manx growled.

"We had all better be good sports," Major Tom said as he approached them, puffing aloud. He stood for a moment and took a deep breath. "They're coming. They want what the Manx has, the TomTom. They're taking the Rani route so they'll be here soon. And they're jolly pissed."

"Shit man," Rani said. She spat on the ground.

"We know," Momma said.

"Fatass liar," Rani squealed.

"Hey, chill guys," Manky said.

"Soon we'll hear Immodium's asshole train approaching," Major Tom said. "What's he call it? The Bowelerator? Oh, yes, Thunderbowel, that's it."

"Yeah, you'll smell him before you see him," Spanky quipped.

The Major leaned to Momma. "By the way, in my eyeglass, I thought I saw that Cockflincher chap standing by Immodium Jack's side."

"I knew it," Rani said. "Turdcoat. Tailbutt will be jealous."

Momma shook her head. "Momma not pleased. Momma will rip his balls off, or sit on his face and suffocate him."

Rani laughed. "How's he breathe through that stupid muzzle anyway?"

"It's his flatulence," Errol said, "and all the bull dust. His gaseous state is known across the six deserts."

"Chwist I thought there were five," Nad said.

Maggie and Manx shook their heads and said in unison, "What a stupid day."

"Well what's we do now's boss? What's we do?"

Manx eyed the two Johoks carefully, and then recalled how Simmons spoke that way. "Momma will have something for you to do, she's got bikes, or you can defend her RV; unless you want to go back to your grubby tribe."

Errol slapped his paws together. "Gimme-gimme-gimme," he said fervently.

Nad shook his head. "Oi'm tired of the tribe. I want what you's wants."

"Tailless one," Momma ushered. "Give me the locator."

"It's Manx," he said. "I told you. Locator is useless till we get some altitude and get it charged up."

"You gotta bad attitude, tom. I ought to lock you with the breeders."

"That cattle haul?" Manx pointed. "You're just as fricked as the rest of us," he said. He spat on the ground.

"Manx!"

He swung about to Rani who glared at him.

"She's your Momma, Rani Fluffiosa. Not mine. And she's certainly pissed you off enough times."

"Momma wants to protect our litter," Rani blurted.

Momma sat upright and glared at Rani from her couch. "Don't."

"Who's litter?"

"Not now, Manx," Rani said.

"Yours? Momma's?"

"No, Manx. Protector Gertrude the Russian Blue's children, and children from the other catgirls. That litter is our future."

"Where?" Manx asked.

"On the triple trailers, at the center of this convoy."

Manx drew a deep sigh. He turned away from the slim leather-clad ragdoll, clenched his Stetson and eyed the dust haze far behind them.

"RV topped," yelled the guard holding the hose.

"You gotta arm them," Manx huffed.

"The toms?" Momma laughed.

"It's your only chance out of this hell."

"I'll consider."

"Consider fast," Manx said as he turned and headed for the Interceptor.

"We'll drive two abreast when we clear the desert crinoids," Momma ordered, "Maggie, arrange your semis and get Gertrude to lead the other."

"You're coming with me," Maggie ordered Spanky as she gripped her Intratec.

"Ahem, you're the boss!"

"And I'm going with Manx," Rani said as she dashed off.

Momma nodded and flicked a switch, and pawed at a joystick controller. A steel pole sprung up from the top of the RV and a mast-mounted camera swung to face the mountain. She moved a slider control to zoom the image on the big screen and panned the horizon. She spotted the road locomotive barreling over the rocky dunes, and the hazy white and brown hulk that was Immodium Jack, standing on the footboard.

"Gear up," Momma ordered. "They're coming."

12: The Road War

"Give me that," Manx said as he pointed to the object in the tool compartment.

Rani handed it to him and stared at the road stretching ahead into haze. "What's it for?"

Manx plugged the small device into the lighter socket and slid out a screen. He tapped a few buttons to show a frequency. He flicked a switch and an image appeared.

Rani nodded.

"Now hooked up to Major Tom's onboard camera," he said as he swung a toggle control, "Immodium's a fair distance behind but will be gaining."

"All this tech and we can't get a TomTom to work," Rani said.

"It's charged now," Manx said as he flung off the hat. But we need to find a hill."

"Pity," Rani said softly. "You look cute in a Stetson."

Manx huffed.

"What's that?" Rani said, looking in her mirror.

"Shit," Manx cursed, "Get your sawed-off ready. Johok scouts on a dune buggy."

"Think Nad know's them?"

Manx glanced at her and reached for his gun. "We've tamed ours."

The buggy with oversized wheels zipped past, three Johoks jeering and firing. The semi-trailer behind wavered slightly but held fast and Manx spotted Spanky's grin behind the wheel.

"This is gonna be a really stupid day," Manx grumbled. He fired again as the buggy launched over the hood of the Interceptor.

A bullet shrilled past and hit the glass of the tractor unit behind them.

A Johok fell out of the dune buggy and landed on the hood, grappling the wiper. The scruffy blood-smeared cat grinned through jagged yellow teeth and fumbled for its gun when Manx fired his. The Johok slid off with a scratchy meow and rolled on the road.

Spanky jerked the semi and felt the Johok bumping underneath. He gripped the wheel, eyeing Maggie's frown. "I got it," he said nervously.

"Right," Maggie nodded slowly.

Spanky clicked a microphone. "Breaker-breaker good budgie, you copy?"

"What do you want?"

"Ahem, just seeing if you guys are okay. One rider left on that thing, he's turning around."

"More behind us," Manx said, looking in the mirror.

Bullets streamed from the passenger window of the semi behind them and Manx watched the dune buggy slow to a halt. He shook his head.

"What?" Rani asked. "Maggie got'im!"

"Waste of bullets," Manx said.

"Okay big shot, what would you do?"

"Aim." Manx said. "One bullet only."

Rani laughed. "You must have one low hanging pair."

"You'd know," Manx said.

Rani blushed and looked away. "More," she said, pointing.

"Not yet," Manx said.

"More," Rani insisted.

"Let them get closer."

"They're firing, Manx."

Spanky clicked the microphone. "Hey there good buddy, our eye in the sky Major Tom tells us the scouts are nearing us lead vehicles. They're ignoring everyone else."

"Wait," Manx said.

"Ten-four my tailless good buddy," Spanky said.

"Quit the CB talk," Manx ordered.

"Why aren't they attacking the other semis, let alone the fuel tankers?" Rani asked.

"They want to cut the head off the snake," Manx said. He eyed the dust swirls approaching.

Bullets rang off the rusted metalwork surrounding the semi behind them.

Spanky held the juddering wheel and Maggie smiled.

"You liking this aren't you."

"Sort of," Spanky said. "Better than being Cockfarter's engineer."

Maggie laughed.

"We shouldn't both be here at the same time," Rani said. "I made a mistake. One of us has to make sure Momma and the nursery are okay."

"She's got it covered." Manx looked at her face turning white and rolled his eyes. He clicked the mike. "Poppa to Momma, you copy?"

Rani cringed. "You serious?"

"I see you got activity up there," Momma replied. "That means Immodium fart buster's getting close. Those Johoks are nothing compared to his Ferals."

"Oi," someone uttered in the background.

Rani yanked the microphone from Manx. "Is that one of the two Johoks? You want me there?"

"It's okay. They're keeping me company..."

Rani laughed.

"...but one of them keeps wanting to go to the john. I'll get the trebuchet ready, if he can handle it."

"He'll love that," Rani said laughing. "He may even dump mid-flight."

Manx smirked at her and something caught his eye. "Duck!" He pushed her down as a biker whizzed past, firing a bullet through one window and out the other.

"I got this," Rani said and fired.

The bike skidded off the road on its side, sparks flying. The Johok biker's head was then whacked by a rock on the side of the road, the helmet coming loose and clattering under a semi wheel.

"Got this," Spanky said, holding the steering wheel straight. "You just put that DC9 to good use."

Maggie looked at the weapon and cringed. She threw it on the back seat and then climbed through the window.

"Wha-what are you doing?" Spanky screeched.

Maggie hung on to the handle outside and waved her boomerang at him. With big green eyes wide open, she grinned. She climbed to the top of the tractor unit.

Manx eyed her in the mirror. "Does she need to do that?"

Maggie lobbed the boomerang. It swept low over the desert plants and swung up to the neck of a Johok rider, slicing the head off. She held out her arm and caught the blade in her thick leather and steel mesh glove.

More riders arrived, some Johoks, others Ferals. They kept pace with the Interceptor and leading semi-trailer. The riders gawked at them and waved their sawed-offs, machine guns, and spears.

Rani nodded slowly. "Look at that stupid big Gatling. Someone's gotta take it down."

"Almost time," Manx said.

A voice screeched over the speaker. "Hey good buddy–"

"Okay Spanky... Now!"

The metal-clad upper panels of their semi swung down and clanged against the side of the truck, covering the wheels. A dozen catgirls started firing upon the riders.

Riders and vehicles swayed and crossed each other's paths in the confusion, some rolling over, their riders falling out like rag dolls, Manx thought.

Someone fired a flare gun from the semi. The sizzling red ball and yellow trail snaked through the scattering Ferals and slammed into a larger buggy beyond. The cats in there jumped up and down as the flare spat and hissed at them. The dune buggy then flipped and the yellow smoke swirled. A Feral got up and jumped and began to run, his ass alight.

"This is gonna be one furry road by the time we're finished," Rani said.

"It ain't over till the fat cat sings," Manx breathed.

"You dissin' Momma?"

Manx smirked at her. "This is too easy. Immodium's relentless."

Rani nodded and eyed the trailing convoy, wondering about Momma.

- - -

"Mmmm, nice rat jerky," she said while chewing.

"Gotta go," Nad whined, holding his legs together.

Momma glared at the Johok as the big screen in the background played out an old movie...

"...Garfield, Garfield!"

"What is it now, Sylvester?"

"Soylent Whikkas is cat, is cat!"

Momma flicked off the screen. "So, Nad, you really hav'ta dump do you?"

"Yes Momma, need to go rool baaad." Nad dropped his pants. "This RV has a can, right? Or I can dump over the side here?"

"You want a bullet in your ass?" Momma sneered at him. "Besides, you'd fall into my can as it's built for my whopping big ginger ass."

Nad nodded.

Momma forced a smile. "We make dung useful in our tribe; for fuel, and for our enemies."

Nad nodded again and smiled nervously. "I ain't forgot the Tray, Momma."

Momma grinned. "Good. Now as you know, the latrine is the last semi-trailer in this convoy. It's well reinforced. It's the last trailer for a good reason. And to get there you need to be launched."

"Dafriq?"

Momma coughed. "If you can launch your bike over a hood, this will be a cinch."

"Sure!" Nad nodded quickly and grinned.

"Just think of this as the same, but by the seat of your grubby pants."

"Uh-huh..." Nad's smile dropped.

"This way," Momma said.

She led him to a large wooden seat at the back of the RV, hanging from the ceiling by three ropes.

"Sit."

Nad nodded and sat on the concave spoon-shaped chair.

Momma flicked a switch and the roofed section at the back of the RV unfolded to open sky.

Nad looked about to see a yellow double-arched support frame before him and a big steel I-beam above and he realized that the sling ropes lead from the beam to his seat. He sniggered.

"What?" Momma asked, glaring at him.

Nad pointed. "Golden arches, same as your door."

Momma sighed and rolled her big eyes. "Now," Momma said. "Consider yourself a payload."

Nad raised a paw–

"And, my dear Johok, there is the counterweight," she said, pointing.

Five guards sitting on a steel chair above waved back at him, grinning.

"Oh shit," Nad said.

Momma held a lever. "Five... When up high, scope the trailer and aim for the landing mattress."

"What?" Nad looked about nervously.

"Four... Put your arms under your legs, look for the landing light – it's a proximity sensor on the latrine – and swing your body so your butt aims at the opening, or you will miss the landing mattress and wind up as road fodder."

"But–"

"Three-two-one!" Momma yanked back the lever. "And let go of the rope," she yelled after him.

The beam swung up fast, flinging the Johok high into the air.

"SHIIIIIIIIIIIIIIIIIIIIIIT..."

Nad watched the semi-trailers skim one-by-one under him and he spotted the last semi and the mattress. A light flashed on the roof of the semi. He crouched, gripping behind his legs tight and swinging about awkwardly as he barreled down through the hatch, slamming onto the edge of the mattress, to bounce onto the hard tread plate floor.

A guard helped him up and smiled crookedly. "Aww, you almost missed da landing bed, furhawk. You a lucky cat."

Nad stood awkwardly and saw a dozen cats waiting at cubicle doors, ready to go, some jumping up and down, others holding their crotches. He saw another cat loading dry dung pellets into cartridges, and mixing in gunpowder.

"What happens when Momma comes?"

The guard folded his arms. "Our union made sure she had her own can." He pointed and said, "Now stand in line."

Momma focused the telescope to the latrine semi and the road beyond. She spotted a dozen cat's asses hanging out the side. "No blood, Errol; your buddy made it."

Errol gulped and kept his legs together.

"That semi is most important," Momma said. "Solid waste that's not used for making a slippery road goes into the special Shatling for the rear gunner. Immodium will hate it. Consider it like a rabbit pellet gun, but much bigger."

"Here come the Feral vehicles," Manx said as he eyed the mirror.

"Johoks were used as fodder," Rani said. "Why they put up with Immodium?"

"Because your Momma saw them as inferior," Manx said.

Rani glared at him and looked to the horizon. "How far you think we have to go?"

"Past The Shells? No idea. The coast could be another five hundred miles, or fifty. Everything has changed."

"What's The Shells anyway?"

"No one knows. They're from the time of World Die. They say the wind howls there like a banshee, amplifies the sounds of the desert."

Manx spotted the CB signal meter clicking and wound up the volume.

"Trailer Three, am landing for supplies. Have fast charger ready."

"Major Tom's picking up some bombs," Rani said.

Manx spotted the quadcopter dropping out of view as it landed on the truck near Momma's RV. "What's he loading with?"

"Grenades," Rani said. "We found them at an old US base."

"Shit, hope they still work," Manx said.

Rani took the microphone. "Gertrude copy?"

The radio replied with static. "Momma copy?"

"I hear you; I sent Gertrude to check the nursery. Make it quick, Rani."

"Momma, ask Gertrude to launch the UAVs as soon as she can. I have a controller with me."

"Okay child," Momma said. "But some are not working. Gertrude's cursing Jock for leaving her."

"*You* sent him away, Momma," Rani yelled.

"Jock was always drunk, and a peeping tom," Momma said. "But I regret the decision. Look, I'm about to send Errol to the Latrine. Nad is flicking his way back on the boards; says he can help me with the drones and also making crinoid desert plant bombs."

"Nice," Manx breathed. "So how to they get back from the latrine? Another catapult?" Manx asked.

"Hate that word," Rani said. "Not a trebuchet, but a springboard, from semi to semi," Rani said quickly. "It's just a big diving board with a spring on the end that flings the occupant sitting on the other end. It hits a steel crossbeam and that's how we hop across road trains while on the move. Works okay unless two use one at the same time and splat each other between trucks. Sometimes we launch onto enemy vehicles, but it never works out. Maggie's semi has a different thing, a metal swing boom, with rope and harness but that swings outwards. We got all this stuff from Clown Chasm."

Manx laughed through a cough. "Suppose Immodium uses ropes, whips, flag poles, chains, and anything else that involves bondage–"

"Watch it!" Rani jerked the wheel off him.

Manx gripped it tighter. "Got it," he breathed. "More frick'n road eaters…"

"Plants," yelled Rani over the CB.

"Ten-four rubber ducky," Spanky replied.

"Shitty plants," Maggie squealed. "This road will be utterly useless in a few years."

"Only a few this time," Rani said, "May be more ahead." She eyed another off-road buggy flip and skittle over. She shook her head. "Dumb furry plants."

"It's a furry road, my good buddy," Spanky yelled over the CB.

"Shit."

"I know Manx; the plants will soon stop us from migrating at all."

"No, I mean Spanky's stupid CB lingo," Manx said.

The gyrocopter droned overhead.

"He's locked and loaded," Rani said looking up, her head out the window.

Manx grabbed her shoulder and tugged her back as a bullet whizzed by.

She looked at him white-faced and then thumbed for bullets.

A UAV mini copter hovered in front of the windshield, the camera panning. Their screen flicked on to show Momma waving at them.

Manx and Rani waved back and then the screen went blank. The mini copter swung off and Rani looked in the mirror. "Blast smoke."

"That was explosion near Momma's," Manx said.

Rani pulled herself through the sunroof and ran back across the roof.

"Wait!"

"Hold your position," Rani yelled as she lunged for the grille guard on the tractor unit behind them.

Maggie stuck her head out. "I heard it too."

"Gimme your DC9...hurry."

Maggie reached for the gun and shot past her at a Feral buggy.

"Thanks." Rani grabbed the machine gun through the window and stuffed it down her belt.

"Release the swing arm," Rani yelled as she climbed down the side of the semi and stood on a platform, gripping the waste-high handle.

"Too much crossfire," Spanky said. "You're as mad as that Manx dude."

"Pull the lever now," Rani shouted as she clipped her rope harness.

Maggie pulled the yellow dash lever down and the side of the semi clanked as the giant pole and knotted line decoupled from the truck, swinging her out past the road's edge. She spotted Gertrude waving at her from the other semi.

Rani aimed the machine gun at the larger dune buggy approaching fast from the desert behind them. She fired a round as the boom arm swung about and slapped the side of the other semi, Rani jumping through the open hatch into the arms of Momma's guards as the other guards fired at the Ferals.

"Three more hauls to get to," Rani gasped at them.

"Can't raise Momma on the radio still," a guard said. "But she'll be fine. You needn't come."

"I need to *know*," Rani said.

In the tractor unit Maggie nodded to Spanky. "We need our own trebuchet."

"Too dangerous," Spanky cried. "And what's *he* doing?"

Manx shot ahead of the convoy and swung about, clicking the microphone and speaking close. "My ride is safer than that stupid shit," he hissed.

Manx shot past them and headed down the line, as the next semi-trailer's boom arm carrying Rani swung outwards, bullets clattering off the steel pole and chewing her harness as she pressed down firing at the Feral riders before falling.

Manx hit the pedal as Rani fell onto the hood. She clambered through the sun roof as another bullet skipped past and ricocheted under the semi beside them, a vent of air hissing onto the road.

"Stop interfering," Rani yelled at him.

"Thanks would be nicer," Manx said flatly. "Now pull your head in."

More bullets clattered off the hood. Manx stepped down on the pedal and headed for Momma's RV.

"Momma," Rani yelled into the microphone.

"Back, Rani; radio antenna now fixed."

"You okay?"

"A gas tank vented and the side blew out. The armor around it held up but we lost one."

"She don't have enough soldiers down there," Manx said. "We should be at the back of the convoy, not the front."

"That's not ours," Rani said and pointed up.

Manx eyed the hovering mini gyrocopter swing past them. "What the... it's got a green furry head on it," Manx said.

"Looks like a sick kitty mask," Rani said.

Immodium slapped his paws together as he watched the drone screen. "Gooood...." He breathed. "My pretties have brought him back from the lead."

Cockflincher took the joystick. "He's about to fire at it."

Manx aimed at the drone and a bullet scraped the back of his paw; his gun flinging out of his paw and clattering on the road.

"Shit!"

"Take the wheel," Manx said to Rani. He reached for an arrow and slung it back on the crossbow and fired. The arrow hit the top side of the furry green face, a grinning cat mask, now with an arrow sticking out of its head. "Steady," he ordered Rani. He fired another shot and the arrow hit the other side of the cat mask head.

"You're a shit shot on the move, Manx," Rani said.

Spanky watched the drone swing down at Manx. "Hey Maggie, that looks like an Android bot, with the two antennas."

"Sure," Maggie said.

"We got'im now," Cockflincher said.

"Keep distracting them," Immodium hissed.

Cockflincher lifted a plastic dash panel with a skull on it and flicked a switch underneath.

Manx watched a nozzle drop down from the underside of the drone.

"Shit!" He swerved the road as the gun fired, the reflex pushing the 'copter upwards.

"Bwahaha," Immodium laughed. "My little rats with wings are working."

"Something Jock made that works?" Cockflincher said.

"He's a good muckle," Immodium breathed. "Get it flying back down again," Immodium said. "I wanna watch 'em burrrn."

Cockflincher flicked another switch and as he watched the screen; a domed metal section partly blocked the onboard camera as it tilted down from the underside.

"Now what," Rani said.

"That's a canister," Manx said.

"A thrower?"

Manx yanked the wheel again and the 'copter kept pace. He slammed the brakes and swerved as a Feral biker launched over the top of them, firing.

The furry drone swung down and fire erupted from its underside.

"Other sawed-off," Rani said, handing it to him.

Manx floored the pedal, swung the gun out the window and fired as he felt the flames singe the side of his bloodied paw.

The drone blew apart.

"Another," Rani pointed.

Manx spotted the furry drone launch what looked like rotten apples at the guards on the cattle-haulers. "How many drones does he have?"

"However many Jock Strappe made."

"Tell me more about Jock."

"Our furgineer… was… our furgineer – Momma caught him getting the girls drunk and banished him."

"He's working for Immodium then," Manx said.

Bullets shrilled overhead.

Manx and Rani looked up as Momma's drone approached and engaged the Feral drone, its modified Uzi rattling as it flew past, the drone in front sparking and spinning to the ground.

Immodium slammed his fist on the loco dash as he watched the circling, crashing image onscreen. "Curse that No-tail." He clicked his microphone. "Bring up the rear!" He farted.

Cockflincher coughed. "Yeah bring up the rear."

"Yes master," crackled a voice over the speaker from a three tiered gun hauler down the line.

Immodium breathed down the voice tube. "You muckle bastard Jock; your drones are failing."

"Aye capt'in', if ye pilots were better trained–"

"Release more drones," he ordered.

Immodium looked Cockflincher square in the eyes. "Time for you to muckle up…ahem buckle up. Launch your trike and go git 'em."

"We're in for a drone war," Rani said.

"What about this shit?" Manx asked as he fired at another Feral buggy.

Rani held the mike. "Momma, we got more drones?"

She looked to the RV and then spotted several mini 'copters rising high off the rear RV roof, and off the roofs of other semi-trailers down the line.

Manx watched the trebuchet fling up from the RV, and Rani spotted one of her soldiers firing mid-flight at a Feral biker below, before landing on the latrine semi-trailer.

"Highsider coming," Manx said; jerking the wheel as the sparking bike clattered past them, the Feral rider howling above the sounds of scraping metal.

"They're coming alongside us," Gertrude's voice squealed through the speaker.

"Momma, it's time for the *Wheel*," Rani said.

The radio went dead. Manx slapped it and it came back on. "Momma?"

Something groaned on the triple semi-trailer beyond the RV and nursery truck. Two rusted steel half-discs lifted up high above the semi-trailer and unfolded to make an immense circle covering the road. Another pair of rusted discs groaned upwards and then unfolded out to reveal steel enclosures that dropped down and clanked onto the lower disc floor; steel doors with slits swung down to click onto locking grooves on the lower floor.

Manx eyed a central column and ladder and spotted several of Momma's soldiers climb the ladder and fan out to their seats. The wheel made a grinding noise and began to rotate slowly and the soldiers opened fire over the companion convoy line, to the Ferals beyond, to the enemy drones, and to the convoy in pursuit.

"Shit me," Manx said. "Clown Chasm?"

"That's the War Wheel," Rani said smugly, "a converted Ferris wheel."

"Now a battery wheel," Manx said slowly. "Nice."

A voice cracked over the radio, "We're very proud."

"Momma!"

"All fine so far but these Ferals breed like ferals. There's so many of 'em."

Manx drove past the RV and nursery truck as the girls waved at them from behind the thick glass. He then swung the Interceptor about, firing into a Feral buggy before swinging back and catching up with the road fleet. He spotted Rani fiddling with a small battery. "What's that for?"

Rani eyed him quickly and clipped a wire from her belt to the terminals. "Hope I don't have to use it."

"Hmm, not long now before Immodium joins us for breakfast," Manx said, "*his* breakfast.

- - -

"Prepare the missile," Immodium screeched down the voice tube.

"You sure it's the right time?" asked Jock. "We only have two of the little bastards and one's all rusted up the side fins."

"You will do as Oi's sez," Immodium hissed. "You stewpid fat fuzzball piece of shit."

Jock gulped. He held the tube and looked about the engine room. He peered through the little windows to the front of the engine and spotted Immodium shaking his head while pacing the forward cab. He looked across the desert to see Cockflincher riding away on the modified buggy, sidewinding the spikey plants.

"I can't tell who's madder," Jock whispered to himself, "shit-faced Immodium or fat Momma... but I'm sure done with catching a whiff of that ugly tom's backside!"

"Well?" Immodium hollered.

"Aye the missile will be primed in a coupla wee min's, oh lord and mastergrater."

Immodium hissed again. He swung about to spot a flicking tail and two tatty paws gripping the handrail, Tailbutt heaving himself into the cabin.

"Ahhh," Immodium breathed. "You missed your lover Cockflincher."

"Wha–?" Tailbutt screwed his face at him. "Took ages to get out of the Tray, I had to give something precious to the big ugly guard at the door–"

"Something precious?" Immodium guffawed and farted. "Cockflincher *will* be jealous!"

"My Handi Wipe, douche!" Tailbutt blurted.

Immodium grabbed him by the neck. "Don't take that tone with me, or Oi's will put you in that steel petticoat meself and sell you to Momma. Sure her toms will luvs ya!" He gripped the voice tube. "Muckle bastard Jock, where's me missile. We's in range?"

Jock covered the voice tube. "I swear that muzzle-faced cat has reached a mental warp 10," he cursed under breath. "Ya gleat big... ah, she's online but she's old, she may not fly, she may explode." Jock gulped. "And I really don' want ta keel my litter," he said quietly.

"What, you stupid muckle?"

Immodium punched some buttons on a panel. "Azimuth set...pitch set...roll...locked in."

"Jus' need a wee adjustment."

Jock eyed the base of the missile in the launch cradle as the bulkhead groaned opened above.

Immodium slammed his paw on the launch button. The missile shot through the opening, filling the cabin with smoke.

"Aw, too late...what about me wee litter?" Jock choked on his words. He kneeled down to examine the wiring loom box at the base of the second missile and unscrewed the housing panel.

"I'll show that ungrateful bastard a thing or two," Jock said as he tore the insulator off a wire with his teeth, and twisted it onto another wire. "Time to abandon ship," he said to himself.

"Get that Scottish Fold to pull his wee finger out," Immodium ordered.

Tailbutt headed down the gangway and flung into the room, spotting Jock's gray tail leaving the other exit to the ramp beyond.

Jock spotted a buggy on the ramp and jumped in, screeching the big tires.

"That's my wheels," Tailbutt cried.

"See you's later, Jimmy," Jock cried. He backed down the ramp, past the hammering connecting rods, almost jamming the back tire into one of the thundering triple coin wheels of the locomotive. He whizzed the buggy about, ducking under fire and then wheel-standing, kicking up enough dust to blind the shooters who became smothered in lingering missile exhaust as the rocket streaked over the spread-out convoy and past the Ferals on bikes and in steel-clad dune buggies ahead.

"Bastard!" Tailbutt screamed after him. "Cockflincher'll get you." He waved to the other Ferals to come alongside as Immodium punched new coordinates into the dash panel.

Tailbutt took the wheel of the thundering loco.

Major Tom swooped low and clicked the microphone. "Incoming, Momma!"

The missile lurched past him causing him to swerve hard and spiral to the road. He gripped the stick back up against his tummy and swooped over the latrine semi, catching a whiff on the way.

Momma stared out of the rear window as the missile approached.

"Fire you bastards," she yelled into the microphone.

The war wheel on the tri-semi trailer groaned as a volley of bullets hailed the missile.

"That thing is still flying – and heading for us," the guard said, wide-eyed.

Momma stared at the approaching nose cone that had two sweptback radar cones mounted either side. "Looks like a Mickey Mouse missile," she said quietly.

"Momma," urged the guard.

Manx squinted to the sun as something caught his eye. "Is that what I think it is?" He lined the Interceptor up beside the RV.

"Shit," Rani cursed. She grabbed the microphone. "Guys, up ahead...full power. Step on it and don't look back."

"Roger, ten-four," Spanky said.

"It's falling short," Rani gasped.

The missile slammed into the horizontal Ferris wheel semi-trailer, exploding the war wheel in a mushroom cloud, splitting the round shooting platform apart. Soldiers, guns and steel sprayed across the road and the semi-trailer jackknifed, falling to its side and skidding before rolling off the road.

Rani gripped her face. "The Litter!"

"It's okay," Manx said as the blue smoke cleared.

"But we just lost our main guns," Rani gasped. "Bastards!"

She looked down the line to see the cattle haul, guns poking through the slits and firing, more Ferals swerving and skipping off the road.

Manx's side window shattered as a bullet screamed behind their necks.

"You bastarrrd!" yelled Cockflincher.

"Not you again; just great," Manx yelled, "so much for bullet-proof."

Rani fired at his fuel tank which spluttered a leak. She fired again and it sparked and exploded, flipping the buggy. Cockflincher flew into the air to thud on the roof of the Interceptor.

A fist flung down through the sunroof.

Manx pressed a button and a whining sound uttered under the hood. "Damn it," he cursed.

Rani grabbed the flying fist and sliced it with a knife just as the fist flicked it out of her hand.

Cockflincher screamed and fired a shot into the vehicle.

The car swerved, whacking the sides of the RV as Manx tried to keep it straight.

A soldier from atop the RV fired at Cockflincher and the bullet skipped off the roof.

Cockflincher's brass knuckled paw flung through the sunroof again, claws out.

Rani probed for the pushbutton on the battery pack clipped to her belt. She undid her leather breast pocket, leaned back as the clawing fist waggled above her, and she pressed the button, a red beam cutting across Cockflincher's wrist.

Cockflincher's curdling scream rang loud into the car.

"What the hell was that?"

"Nothing, Manx," she said quickly as she zipped her jacket up.

Manx looked at her oddly and she grinned.

Bullets rained through the roof.

"Take the wheel," Manx said to Rani.

Manx squirmed across the seat as Cockflincher's bloody paws grabbed onto his collar and hauled him through the sunroof.

Manx swung at the tall tom.

"Missed, pretty boy," Cockflincher said.

More soldiers atop the RV trained their guns on the fighting toms.

"I knows you, Manx. I was just a kitty when Tailcutter groomed me."

Manx sliced a right into his gut and pulled a knife from his boot, slashing his knee.

Tailcutter screeched and then laughed. "Ya missed my business by an inch." He hissed through his clenched teeth and then laughed.

"*Where* is Tailcutter?" Manx demanded. "I want my tail back!"

Cockflincher laughed, "Why, it'd be incy wincy, you dumb bastard. What, you gonna graft that back onto your sorry ass?" He swung the brass back of his leathered paw across Manx's face. Blood gashed into the cabin.

Manx latched his bloody paws around Cockflincher's neck. "It's… not about the tail," he said, squeezing.

"It's about revenge," Rani growled from the driver's seat.

"What?" Manx glanced down at her holding the wheel.

A brass-knuckled fist flew into his face and he fell back on the Interceptor roof as the vehicles sped through smoke, blood, and bullets.

Manx lay on his back and Cockflincher threw himself on top of him.

"It's WWF time, No-tail," Cockflincher breathed.

"Sorry, already donated," Manx said as he thrust his knee into Cockflincher's groin.

Cockflincher fell back in pain and grabbed his crotch. "My business!" he cried.

Manx crouched back, flicking his legs in the air and thrusting both boots into Cockflincher's guts.

Cockflincher flung backwards down the windshield, swinging about, reaching for the wiper blade, blood flying from his wrist where Rani had laser cut it. He breathed heavily, fogging up the windshield as Rani jerked the car.

"Immodium knows where Tailcutter is," Cockflincher cried as he slid back down the hood and slipped out of sight.

The Interceptor vaulted as Rani felt the bumps underneath and then watched the RV beside them bounce for a moment.

"And to think Momma trusted that ass," Rani said as Manx clambered through the sunroof, his face bloodied. "She should have neutered him years ago."

"Immodium knows." Manx huffed as he wiped his face.

Rani eyed him. "Forget that sick bastard. I'll keep driving," she said.

"Fine."

Major Tom's voice rattled over the speaker, "The other vehicles have negotiated the fallen soldier semi but it's slowed them back down the line from the rest of us. They need to catch up with us fast."

"They need to pick up survivors," Manx said.

"But that jolly ugly Feral loco monster is closing," Major Tom said.

Manx sneered. "What, the train or Immodium?"

Rani looked up to see Momma pressing her face against the glass, nodding.

"Let's go."

She veered the Interceptor off the road, cutting off another stray biker firing at them. The bike rolled under the Litter semi which jolted.

Manx heard some muffled screams from inside the trailer as they passed and he spotted a row of small wide-eyed faces staring outside, some Persian, others ginger, gray, and black and white.

"They got another gleat nasty missile," a faint Scottish voice crackled over the radio.

Manx wound up the RF gain on the CB. "Who the hell is this?"

"It's Jock!" Rani squealed.

"Oh-em-gee!" they heard someone cry over the radio.

"That's Gertrude," Rani said. "Jock's her sire." She beamed at him and squeezed his arm.

"Uh-huh." Manx looked ahead. He then took the mike. "*What* other missile."

"I'm on this wretched buggy, coming from your five o'clock," Jock said. "So don't shoot!"

Rani snatched the microphone back. "What about the bloody missile?"

"I rigged it to explode," Jock said. "It'll be a real beauty. As soon as that sick bastard Jack hits the launch button–"

"You better hurry up then; go to the front, help Momma out," Manx said. "There." He pointed and said, "The stragglers."

Rani handed him the monocular.

"Rear tanker is refueling the latrine, and the cattle-hauls are moving ahead," Manx said. "They better hurry up; I can see a weird train behind them with a stupid cat skull on it."

"That's Immodium's converted road train," Rani said, "the Thunderball. I hear you destroyed his other loco, the Cattanooga choo choo. No wonder he's pissed with you."

"Yeah, we clowned around with it," Manx said.

Rani smiled.

"Hit the floor; let's see if we can speed things up."

Rani raced the Interceptor down the road to the last trailers and swerved the car to align with the tanker driver.

"What's happening?" Manx yelled out the window.

"This tanker not empty yet. But have refueled the semis now," the black and white tom replied as he held the wheel.

"Let it go," Manx said. "Stop here and get in, we'll take you to the latrine semi."

"Why?"

"Just do it," Rani said.

The driver stopped his tanker and climbed out, as the Interceptor pulled up. He squeezed into the back of the Interceptor. "I hate the latrine," he said.

"Well it's better than being left for shit here," Manx said.

Rani revved up and Manx threw a lit match to the decoupled hose that spewed fuel onto the road.

The road and hose lit up as they skidded away.

The driver looked back to watch the tanker explode.

"That'll slow them down," Manx said.

Rani eyed the mirror. "Ah, I don't think so," she said nervously.

A giant gleaming gray skull face pushed the black smoke and flames aside, the loco whistling as it ploughed through the tanker, crushing it as it kept rolling towards them.

"Shit, that's a big train," Manx said.

"I don't wanna catch that train," Rani said quickly. "Where'd he get the skull head?" she asked.

Immodium clutched the wheel and laughed beside Tailbutt.

"Oi'm's gonna eat you's alive!" Immodium screamed. "You's lot is so frickin' fried!"

- - -

"What's that thing ahead of us?" Maggie pointed.

"It's shimmering," Spanky said, "Is it that Golden City?" He looked in the mirror to spot the rest of the convoy much further back, amidst a smoke haze and trails of dust and ash filling the sky. "Shit, looks bad back there."

"Momma should have put the young ones with us," Maggie said.

Spanky laughed. "It's not safe anywhere, except back at the mountain."

"Too late for that," Maggie said.

"Uh-oh," Spanky said as he tapped the fuel gauge. "This rig is getting low."

"Where's the other tanker-trailer?" Maggie asked as she stuck her head out the window.

"Can't see it," Spanky said. "And I can't get the drone to work to find out; the image is blocky, the joystick does nothing."

"Could be half-dead on the sand; it's such a mess back there."

The vehicle slowed.

"We can't stop now, Spanky, Momma gave us orders."

"Fuel's lower than I thought," Spanky said nervously. He waved his arm out the window to Gertrude's truck which seemed to hang back from the front of the line, and then clicked the mike. "Gertrude, blue buddy, you copy?"

"Low on fuel," she replied.

Maggie eyed the shell-shaped buildings in the distance. "Take us there," she said, pointing, "As far as you can."

"Gertrude, see The Shells? We'll meet you there."

"I can make it, Spanky. But where's Jock?"

"Right behind you lass," a voice crackled over the speaker. "I passed the convoy, and what a mess back there. But I took out three Ferals trying to jump on Momma's RV; shot them with this trusty rusty MG-8 machine barrel while driving this blasted jerky contraption at the same time. And you know sumth'n', I saw Momma blow me a kiss."

"Lucky you," Spanky said.

"I heard that," Gertrude said.

"We're getting close to those weird buildings," Spanky said. "Why is the ground ahead shimmering?"

"Why are we jerking Spanky? You tapping the brakes?"

"No!"

The semi-trailer juddered and the horizon appeared to dip.

Spanky stopped the truck and jumped onto the road. "Shit, tires sinking into the asphalt, Maggie. Look at all these plants; they've eaten all of this road, and the ground below, it's wet!"

Gertrude's semi stopped behind them, as did the few doubles behind them.

A large dune buggy flew over the road and sloshed into the mushy sand beyond; wheeling up sprays of sand, rocks and water as it spun about and screeched to a halt.

"Jock!"

Jock clambered out and rushed to Gertrude's side.

"Water table must be high here," Maggie said. "The road looks fricked."

Spanky spotted the gyrocopter and waved to Major Tom to land. He put paws on hips and stared back down the road to the hazy blazing melee approaching them. "We're screwed."

13: The Sinkhole

"We're gaining, Tailbutt!" Immodium gripped his shoulders and breathed into his face.

"Shit boss, can't tell which end is breathing."

Immodium Jack ignored him and pulled the whistle. "More power," he yelled into the voice tube.

A timid voice replied, "Yes master!"

"Is that Jello?" Tailbutt asked.

"That black 'n white may be way fatter than Jock but he's loyal. He's my Jellicle cat!"

"Ah, I get it, he's from Tennessee."

Immodium laughed.

"Ahem, if I recall, he can't really fit in the cab," Tailbutt said as he looked back down the engine. He spotted the black and white cat's fur, sides and ears poking through the open windows. "I can't see his face. Jeez, he's real big in'he."

"Be nice to my Jello," Tailbutt breathed. "Not everyone can be as lean as me."

"Or stink so," Tailbutt said under breath.

Immodium caught sight of the Interceptor driving past a latrine semi up ahead of them. And then he released a long squealing fart.

Suddenly the back of the latrine semi opened, clanging onto the road. A brown slush gushed onto the road and then a bulbous gun on an iron pivot started firing, the barrel rotating slowly.

Tailbutt gripped his face. "Shit! It's shit!"

"A Shatling gun," Immodium said as he laughed and then yelled over a megaphone, "You thinks my loco will slip on your tiny butt shits?"

"That's a lot," Tailbutt said. "What the hell do they eat?"

The loco raced over the sludge, the triple coin wheels slicing the spinning defecation into the air, which then splattered down the sides of the engine and railcars beyond. All the toms with guns hanging out of their windows instantly flung themselves inside and slammed the windows shut.

"It's missile time," Immodium breathed.

"Target acquired, Boss," Tailbutt said as he covered his nose with a handkerchief while punching some buttons. "Interceptor locked on."

"That train is getting shittingly close," Rani said.

Bullets rang overhead.

"Hey, Fluffiosa," someone cried over the radio. "You gotta see this."

"Not now Spanky, we're busy."

Immodium slammed his paw onto the Missile Two launch button.

Something sparked under the dash.

"Noooo!" Immodium screamed. "That blasted muckle Jock Strappe has cheated me!"

Tailbutt crawled between Immodium's legs to examine the wiring under the dash. "Please don't fart," he whispered urgently, "please don't fart."

Immodium crouched down and watched Tailbutt fiddle with the wires.

"Ah, think I got it," Tailbutt said as he held up two wires. Something sparked and smoked under the dash.

Immodium staggered back, agape, looked quickly about the cabin, then clicked a timer to ten seconds and pulled down a lever. He rushed out to the front of the train and grabbed a rope.

"Where you going, boss?" Tailbutt asked as he joined the wires.

The rear cabin exploded, ripping the engine apart, the wake racing up the steam chamber into the gas engine, the boiler tubes hissing and casings flaying outwards, the wheels flying apart, the rear bogie and side rods twisting and shredding as the engine blew apart, lifting every carriage off the road behind them, the loco engine tilting on its skull-wedge nose.

A shard of hot metal ripped through Tailbutt's paw, separating it from his arm as he screamed at the exploding mass about to hit him at full force as he jumped.

And then the road began to crack apart and collapse under the convoy.

"Shit Rani, step on it," Manx yelled as he watched the road disintegrate behind them, the immense Feral train smashing down through asphalt, silt, and rock into an enormous sinkhole.

Manx gripped Rani's leg. "Okay… ahem, the edge of the road is still chasing us," he said calmly.

"I can see it," Rani said, gritting her teeth. She probed under the dash and swung down a panel of switches.

Manx frowned at her. "Left two first–"

"–far right ones and then middle two," Rani said quickly as she flicked each switch in the sequence, the LEDs glowing with each throw.

Manx huffed, and then raised a slight smile.

The Interceptor dashed away, pressing them snug into their seats.

A gush of silt, metal shards, and water spewed up into the sky as backwash from the newly-formed chasm where the Feral road train had fallen.

Rani kept her foot down as they left the smoking hole behind them.

"You sussed the Interceptor quick."

Rani squeezed his leg. "Of course."

Manx stuck his head out. "Can't see a train, or any Feral vehicle at all back there."

- - -

Momma ambled out of the RV as it screeched to a halt behind the leading semi. She smiled as the Nursery truck arrived behind them. She kicked a clump of asphalt on the degraded highway. "End of the road?"

"Looks that way," Spanky said. "All mangled beyond."

"End of the road for them too?" Gertrude asked.

They stood on the broken road and stared back at the smoke filling the sky.

"That was one hell of a blast," Maggie said. "Look! Here they come."

The other semi-trailers came into sight and Momma squinted to spot the Interceptor between them.

"The sand's wet here," Gertrude said. "Looks muddy everywhere."

"I was right all along; the water table is washing everything away – every last bit of evidence of kittykind."

"Except that, Momma," Spanky said, pointing to The Shells.

"I say, this has been a dastardly day. What do we do now?"

"You can't go back to the mountain," Manx said as he pulled up. "The Ferals are gone. Their road train fell into a sinkhole, took the lot of them."

"All we can do now is sleep on it then," The Major said.

"We can do more than that," Momma said quietly to the Major. She stared into the shiny horizon past The Shells.

"What is it?" Rani asked.

Momma glanced at Major Tom. "Gather the toms from the haul; get them to inspect all the compression tanks on the ends of each vehicle chassis. Make sure all the expansion gear is intact... just in case."

"I wish Jock was with us to oversee his design," Major Tom grumbled.

Manx cringed. "What's that about?"

Rani took Manx aside. "Let's check out The Shells."

Manx eyed her carefully and glanced at Momma. "You know how cold it gets at night."

Rani gripped his arm as a guard handed her a bag. "Supplies, see? And I know we can find warmth."

Manx smiled. "We'll have to walk it."

"Go, tailless one, and protect her." Momma waved. "Go investigate; not like we gonna do much here, except party!" She grinned.

They turned for The Shells when Gertrude whistled at them, and threw a walkie talkie and flashlight, both wrapped in solar cloth.

Manx caught and pocketed them, and then tapped his left breast pocket for the TomTom. He took Rani's arm as they stepped off the road.

"Few hundred yards and we'll be there," he said.

Rani smiled as they walked into the night.

- - -

The smoke eased off as the chasm flashed from sparks, explosions and the hissing of oil drums in a waft of steam mixed with settling silt. The new chasm edge was jagged where the road had broken away.

A blood-smeared charcoal white paw gripped the asphalt edge. Immodium Jack heaved himself onto the road and rolled onto his back, gasping at the night sky for air as he whisked off his muzzle. He felt the cold blood sticking to the fur on his arm. He groaned and then coughed and shook the dust filter before slotting it back into his tooth muzzle. His face flickered from stark white to yellow as he watched the flames below; before he fixed his muzzle back on.

"It ain't over till the fat pussy sings, and Notail has his last scream," he breathed, "to *my* tune."

And then he farted.

14: The Shells

"Wow," Rani said as they approached the shell-shaped buildings.

"That was a longer walk than I thought," Manx said. "This place is huge. We better stay the night here."

"That's the idea," Rani said, smiling.

The made their way up a stone and tiled rampart covered in shattered glass, the paving beneath cracked and broken away. Manx touched the side of the shell-like building and some tiles flaked off under his paw.

They struggled through a set of twisted broken glass doors, covered in seaweed, barnacles, and sand.

"What is this place?"

"I have a faint memory of this building," Manx said slowly, "from childhood. But it doesn't seem to be in the right place."

"Right place?"

"A city by the ocean," Manx said.

Their voices echoed around what looked like a torn-apart lobby, as they approached a large chamber beyond that shimmered in the moonlight.

Manx looked up to massive sheets of angled glass, some sections broken. Water trickled down curved glass sections and pattered onto the floor. A water droplet touched his paw and he sucked on it and then spat it out.

"Smells like the sea here," Rani said.

"Sounds like listening to a conch shell; I vaguely remember that too," Manx said quietly, eyes agog at the huge supporting beams and glassed sections. "I think this used to be two buildings. Frick knows what happened to the other half."

Rani rubbed her hands together.

Manx motioned to her. "Let's find a warmer place to rest."

They stepped over some brass pipes of different lengths scattered across the floor.

"What are these?"

"Organ pipes," Manx said, "though I don't know how I remembered that either."

"Could make useful mortar launchers or barrels," Rani said.

They climbed some stairs and entered a hallway, and pushed open a door hanging loose by one hinge.

"What's that name on the door?"

"Batty Humphries," Manx read aloud.

"Who's that?"

"Dunno, keep an eye out," he looked up, "maybe the guy's hangin' off the rafters, ready to crap on us."

"Look, a couch."

Manx picked up some broken pieces of furniture, broke others into smaller pieces, tore off some fabric covers and stuffed it all into a rusted trash can, and lit it.

They flopped on the couch and warmed their paws and Manx fell back and fiddled with the TomTom.

"It's coming on."

They watched the small screen glow their faces. Manx pressed a scan button. "Must be right time for satellite overpass," he said, "'cos the signal is clear."

"But what are we looking at?"

An image of a spread-out ocean city flickered onscreen.

"Is this that Golden City Immodium and Momma want?" Manx asked. "Don't look golden to me."

"She never spoke about it," Rani said, "Just that it's probably the last place on earth to live and raise kittens."

Manx nodded. "Signal's good; wonder how far away it is."

"We can't get there now," Rani said. "The road's wrecked beyond repair and there are desert plants everywhere."

"I heard the Fluffiosas never give up," Manx said flatly. "At least you know how to make cheap biofuel now."

"There you go again; caring, when you pretend you don't."

"I lost everything," Manx said. "Not just my tail, my whole life went to hell because of Tailcutter; my wife, my family, all my friends... gone."

"We've all lost something." Rani stared into his big orange eyes. "As a people we have lost something."

"You okay? Or is that crease on your forehead trying to tell me more?"

"You're talking too much," Rani said as she stared into his eyes. "So unlike you..." She gripped his collar and brought her lips to his.

Manx hesitated, and then planted his lips onto hers as their whiskers twitched together. He held her closer; she wrapped her arms around his neck and purred.

"Ooh, you haven't lost your tail after all," Rani said.

Manx sat back and took off his leather jacket.

Rani spotted a dozen scars in his side, where no fur showed. She ran her paw over a tattoo on his side of two snakes arranged in the shape of the letter T, one snake biting the middle of the other.

"Tailcutter's signature," Manx said.

Rani gently pressed her paw there for a moment while looking into his eyes.

Manx pulled the zipper of her jacket down and she took his paw.

"What?"

Rani sighed and hesitated. "Here." She unzipped to reveal a leather-clad metal dome covering her breast, held by a harness.

Manx sat up and stared at it. A light flickered in his eyes. He held his paw to the breast plate, gently touching the curved metalwork and join studs, running his finger to a diamond nipple. "Nice laser focus," he said slowly.

And then he saw a tear emerge from her eye.

"I… had cancer," she said slowly. "They cut away my breast, but Jock added this laser contraption and you know something, I actually like it, even if it sucks the battery. I only get two goes per charge."

"Come here," he said, and embraced her.

"You don't mind?" she asked.

"Of course not."

"All the toms rejected me. That's why Momma was so protective. I'm surprised she let us go here alone."

Manx looked into her eyes as she zip-closed her jacket. "I could modify that to make one helluva headlight."

She smiled and gazed into his eyes longingly and they embraced again, sprawling across the old couch to kiss and cuddle by the burning trash can, until finally falling asleep.

- - -

Manx shuddered as the severed bloody head was held before him, Tailcutter's buddies pinning Manx's eyes back to witness her stone cold eyes and a scream frozen in time as their home was doused in gasoline.

"Josie," he mumbled. He kicked as Tailcutter hissed into his ear. The hissing grew louder. Manx kicked harder and struggled as the hissing rang through his ears like rippling static from a detuned radio–

"Manx! Wake up!" Rani shook him and he fell off the couch.

He slowly opened his eyes to Rani and held up his paw against the morning sun.

"You must have had one bad dream," she said. "Josie… your wife?"

"Yes." Manx cupped his ears for a moment. "That hissing...you hear it?"

"Nuh-uh," Rani said.

The radio fizzled, "Come in, Fluffiosa, Spanky here."

Manx probed his pocket and produced the transceiver, handing it to Rani.

"You guys okay?" she asked.

"We got a problem," Spanky said. "Momma wants you back here right now."

"Why?"

"Wherever you are in that shell building, take a look out the window, away from our position."

Manx and Rani stood up and looked outside.

She gripped the radio, holding it flat to her ear. "What? I don't see anything, except the hills in the distance."

"They're not hills," Momma screeched into the radio.

Manx reached for his belt and pulled out the monocular. "Funny hills… they're moving…"

"I don't like this," Rani said as she tugged at his jacket.

"They're right," Manx said as he collapsed his scope. "That hissing noise, now rumbling. Can't you hear it? It's water."

"What?"

"That's a frick'n' king tide. Let's go."

"But we'd be safer here wouldn't we?"

"Come back," Spanky yelled through the speaker. "Momma's readying the inflatable pontoons."

"What the hell?"

"Right," Rani said as she clasped her face. "You asked about the compressed air canisters under our semis.

Momma got Jock to design blowout inflatable supports for the trucks in case of floods."

"You kidding me. How do you propel that?"

"We don't," Rani said with a sad look on her face, except for the buggies. "Jock was supposed to build rotors, but, you know, Momma's pride butted in, the same pride that played around with me and Maggie."

Manx grabbed her arm and they headed into the corridor and down the stairs. He glanced outside and saw the water hills closer and higher.

Something moved out of sight.

Manx turned and felt cold metal whack across his back. He fell over; the walkie talkie clattered onto the floor.

"Manx!" Rani screeched.

He looked up to see Immodium standing over him, holding an organ pipe.

"You happy to see me?" Manx asked as he blindly groped for the radio.

"You killed my tribe," Immodium hissed.

"No, it was Jock actually," Rani said.

Immodium swung about to aim the pipe at Rani, and then swung it back at Manx.

Manx dodged the pipe as it clanged to the floor next to his head. He grabbed the radio and yelled into it, "Come get Rani, quick–"

Immodium knocked the radio out of his hand and Manx crawled backwards across broken glass. He glanced at Rani. "Go!"

Manx probed the floor behind him and felt a rod and gripped it. He swung it up to see that it was a shorter length of organ pipe.

Immodium laughed. "Mine's bigger than yours," he breathed heavily as he swung the pipe.

Manx sprung up. "Let's see what's behind your stupid muzzle," he said as he took a swing.

Immodium ducked, and swung his pipe back up to Manx's groin.

"Manx!" Rani squealed.

Manx dropped the pipe and fell to the floor; he yelled to her, "I said go; leave *now!*"

"Not so fast," Immodium hissed after her.

"Gutless bastard," Manx yelled as Immodium grabbed Rani's collar. "Let her go you big lump of stinking shit. My god but you stink."

Immodium flung Rani against a wall and about-faced and stomped back towards Manx. "No one calls me gutless, no one! Just because I have a flatulence problem...I'm the tyrant everyone needs. I'm the tyrant who'll take your TomTom, and make the Golden City the Feral City." He reached out towards Manx, one paw open, the other swinging the organ pipe.

Manx kicked back, grabbed his organ pipe and lifted the pointy end up as Immodium lunged at him; the pipe piercing straight through Immodium's filthy jacket and into his stomach.

Immodium dropped his pipe which clanged on the floor as Rani struggled to stand, holding her head.

Immodium's sodden face turned white and he grabbed the ingressed pipe with both paws, staggering back. He clenched his teeth and growled and pulled the pipe out slowly, his eyes opening wide as he grinned back at them.

"Frickun hell!" Rani gasped.

"What the hell are you?" Manx asked, "A zombie? No one could survive that."

Immodium burst out laughing as he withdrew the pipe from his guts. "Years ago, I had a gastrectomy; my organs were rearranged and the doctor left a big gap in my guts, but I killed the doctor anyway because I still kept flatulating," He broke into laughter, "Dropping my guts!"

Manx and Rani stared at each other wide-eyed.

Manx then grinned slightly. "So you're gutless after all. And that explains the oversized raggy diapers you're wearing on the outside."

"Manx," Rani urged.

"How often do you change them, you big ugly douche?"

"How darrrre youuuu..." Immodium bellowed as he stomped. "Time to take a dump on you."

"No you don't," Manx said as he got up quickly.

Immodium loosened his belt.

"Oh gross," Rani said. She looked out the window. "That wave is huge now!"

Manx ignored her as he watched Immodium stomp towards him, arms outstretched, one paw swinging the bloodied pipe.

Rani jumped on Immodium's back and held his arms down. She pressed her thumb down on his wrist and he dropped the pipe.

Immodium staggered.

"You're losing blood, you fecal feral," Manx said.

Immodium's eyes rolled back to their whites.

Manx flicked off Immodium's muzzle and for a moment gaped at the soft white fur underneath, and Immodium's deep blue eyes. He gripped Immodium's sodden white neck. "Tailcutter...where is that bastard? Flincher told me you know."

Immodium chuckled and spat out blood in his face. "Tailbutt wants his paw back," he gurgled.

"I want my tail back! Tell me where Tailcutter is!"

"I knows where he is," Immodium hissed and spat as his eyes rolled back to glare at him.

"Tell me!" Manx squeezed his grip.

"Tell him," Rani yelled as she wrestled to hold his struggling arms, but feeling the strength diminishing.

"Tell me *now*," Manx urged.

"Why?" Immodium coughed and spluttered, "You're a Manx, you *really* are a Manx, Manx," Immodium gasped hard as he staggered.

"What?" Manx cringed at Rani. "What's he saying?"

"That you really are a Manx?" Rani asked, her face going white.

Manx shrugged.

"And thereby hangs a tale," Immodium choked on the words, as the blood seeped through the fur on his neck, his eyes turning to steel as he squealed out one final elongated fart.

"This is one helluva post apoocalypse," Manx said flatly.

Rani jumped down and Manx stood before Immodium, watching the tyrant's face smirk at him as the last hint of color dissolved from his eyes.

The ground shook under them.

"It's too late," Rani said glancing outside. "There's a big wall of water about to hit us."

The water slammed against the glass and sprayed around the edges of the shell building which groaned and tilted.

They held their arms up but the water washed over the building without breaking through.

They fell back against a wall as the floor lifted and Manx flung out his arm to the sliding walkie talkie. He clicked the button. "Hope you guys didn't come–"

"Yes we did," someone spoke from behind.

"Spanky! Maggie!" Rani cried.

"Wow, this some shit place," Spanky said as he looked about. "Entrance is flooding with water; we gotta go high as possible."

The radio beeped, Momma's voice coming through clear, "Stay there, we're fine, our semis are on pontoons," she said. "It's rough but we'll ride this out."

"C'mon," Manx said as held out his arm.

Rani pressed her face against the glass and watched the semi's on their pontoons being tossed in choppy waters, and carried away from them. "Wow, the road train is now a sea fleet!"

"Come."

She took Manx's hand and they ran up the steps, opening a door to a gangway leading to the top of the shell building.

"No windows up here," Spanky said. "And I'm not going to open that metal door," he said, pointing to the bulkhead above them.

"Good thinking," Manx said firmly. "They'll be back; tide has to go out too."

"But we're nowhere near the ocean," Rani said.

"I couldn't see a beach for miles," Manx said, "Never heard of a tide this big. This is a new world."

"We got a buggy," Spanky said, "we can go when the water drops."

"Could be a while," Manx huffed. "And how's a buggy float? Did Momma make inflatable rubber ducky tires for them?"

"How's you know?" Maggie asked with a smile.

Manx frowned. "Hope you secured it well out there."

"On a long rope," Spanky said, "Hard to sink. Engine's watertight. Momma thinks of everything."

"Don't tell Jock that," Rani said.

Manx listened to the water lapping the lower rooms and said, "Sound is different, quieter, we can move soon and make it back to," he chuckled, "the boats."

Maggie rolled her eyes.

"You two," Rani waved at them, "seem close."

Spanky took Maggie's arm. "We-ell…"

She elbowed him.

Manx sighed. "Now, we wait it out."

15: Desert Sea

"We been swept a mite back from them," Jock said as he held Gertrude's paw. "This trailer had better hold out a wee longer."

"You did a good job with these," Momma said.

"You oughta thank the toms too you know," Jock said.

Momma nodded. "I didn't want anyone to know what they were doing," she said. "People just thought I caged them up for mass breeding."

"Well I did," Gertrude said as she spat on the ground and glared at Momma.

"Hey you canny kitty, you sure you nort got a tad Scorrrt in ya, lass?"

Momma laughed. She eyed the other semi-trailers floating on the massive expanded pontoons.

"That one's sinking now," Gertrude said as she pointed.

"Glad Nad and Errol evacuated that truck, the underside compressors where damaged in our little war."

"Those Johoks have sure become a coupla tame toms," Jock said.

Momma nodded as she watched Major Tom hurrying about the quadcopter, draping tarps and panels over the batteries as the craft teetered on the makeshift deck beside the semi-trailer.

A bullet pinged the exhaust pipe on the tractor unit.

"Shit!" Gertrude grabbed her gun.

"They'll shoot the floats," Jock said. "Momma, don't–"

Momma climbed atop the tractor unit and swung about to see a Feral clinging to an oil drum floating towards them. "Just one," she yelled as another bullet skipped past her whiskers.

"Down from there ya clazy kitty," Jock ordered.

"I don't get you, Jock," Momma said.

"He's trying to help," Gertrude said as she climbed up the side of the semi.

Another bullet flew past.

Gertrude ducked and something caught her eye. "Ohhhh shiiiit… –big wave coming!"

More bullets screeched past them and Gertrude swung about to see the large makeshift dune buggy chopping through the waters like a paddle steamer, the big wheels splashing slowly, Manx and Rani waving at them, Spanky pressing the horn.

Maggie stood behind them, firing her machine gun at the lone Feral on the oil drum.

"That Feral's Tailbutt," Momma said. "Firing left-handed…"

"Huh?"

"Explains the lousy shots, Gertrude," she said.

Momma adjusted her scope. "His right arm is wrapped in bloody cloth… the paw… looks gone."

"Aye I bet he's pissed a hoot," Jock said. He looked about the makeshift barges and floats supporting the heavy vehicles. "Don't know if we can survive another big wave," he said, "We may topple over this time."

The wave rose them up and more bullets rang down upon them as they watched Tailbutt's oil drum rise higher on the crest.

Spanky rode the buggy up the ramp of the closest semi-trailer pontoon barge.

"Here she blows," Jock yelled as the waved lifted them.

"Can't see the Feral," Gertrude cried.

Manx caught a glimpse and fired at the Feral as he ducked the return fire.

A bullet penetrated the massive air-filled bladder below them. Air whistled out.

Momma howled. "Not now!"

Manx and Rani tilted their heads back as the crest of the wave lifted, blocking out sun, their faces going pallid, Jock heaving overboard as he clung to the tie-downs, the water gushing past him.

"I hate water!" Momma cried as she struggled into the RV hold and pushed a button to close the roofed section.

"I hate barfin'," Jock yelled.

Manx and Rani struggled into the tractor unit cabin as it jolted on the massive pontoon, the water bashing down upon them.

Spanky flicked the wiper switch.

Maggie looked at him oddly. "Duh."

The massive wave crashed and tumbled the vehicles and floats, rolling the convoy together as Jock ducked when the RV slammed the side of their trailer.

Manx stuck his head out the window. "Can't see the Feral."

Rani gripped his arm. "Water's getting faster–"

"But wave is settling," he replied as they felt their vehicle pontoons race away, past The Shells, past cliffs and massive boulders.

"Where're we going?" Rani cried.

Manx held her close.

Something whip-snapped behind them.

He flung about to see the heavy rope snatch straps that latched the Interceptor down to the metal ramp tear away and fling apart, the car sliding down the ramp at the back of the semi, the rear dipping into the water.

Manx held her tight and stared into her wild blue eyes, and quietly said, "This is it."

16: A New Coast

Manx sprung upright on the sand as something swooped low over him.

The creature screeched and landed beside them.

Rani rubbed her eyes. "Seagulls!" she squealed. She eyed Jock and Gertrude in the distance, picking up pieces of wreckage.

Jock kicked a tire, half sunk into the sand.

The waves lapped up to their feet and Manx stared to the hazy horizon; a glittering orange-yellow sea under a bluish-yellow sky, ragged hills on either side arcing into the distance where waves crashed upon the rocks, sending their spindrifts high into the air.

And then he saw the Interceptor, partly buried in the sand. He struggled to stand up and looked about the beach.

"Wrecked," Momma said as she held her face, gawking at the half-buried convoy, the pontoons and floats all ripped apart and crumpled.

"But the Nursery survived," Gertrude said as she brought some children with her, hand-in-hand, while others ran about her side, some flicking sand at each other and meowing with delight, others laughing.

Rani released a big sigh. "You think Tailbutt survived?"

Manx shrugged and stared at his vehicle.

"Come with us," Rani said softly as she took his arm.

Manx drew a deep breath, and turned to look into her eyes which reflected the setting sun.

"Hey, over there," Spanky cried. "Did I see lights?"

"The city? Momma said quickly.

"The gyros and blades are wrecked beyond repair," Major Tom said as he skipped down a sand dune, the twisted copter blades jutting out from the sand behind him.

Manx probed for the TomTom and flicked it on. "It's here, that city is here."

"Where?" Maggie said, looking around.

The gulls cried around them, circling and landing on the tilted, wrecked semi-trailers.

"Everything will be spoiled," Momma said and sighed. She stood upright, paws on hips and swished her frizzed ginger tail. "This way..." She waved for them to follow. "Up the hill, everyone."

"Us too I hope," Nad said as he dusted the sand off his torn leathers.

"Yeah us too," Errol repeated as he ran up behind Nad, panting. "Jeez I hate sand down there," he said, pawing at his groin.

"C'mon," Momma said.

Manx nodded and as the tribe wandered up the craggy hillside; he looked back to the water and the scattered wrecks of their convoy littered up and down the beach. The cattle hauls were smashed, but he saw many toms, some holding weapons, and Momma's soldiers ushering others.

"We're lucky," Rani said. "Lots of us survived, thanks to Momma."

"Don't forget Jock, and the Major, and Spanky and Maggie, and a whole bunch of folk including those Johoks," he said.

"And you." Rani squeezed his arm. "But where to now?"

Manx nodded in the direction of the lights and he held up his monocular. "It's a city alright, of some sort, water all around it as far as I can see, and there's a high bridge leading into it; you just have to find where the bridge touches the shoreline and… you're home."

Rani smiled and threw herself at him, squeezing hard.

"Careful, I may fart."

She slapped his side and grinned, her eyes glowing in the sunset.

Momma waved to Rani and the others to follow and they made their way across the ridge towards the lights, the outlines of buildings taking shape as the sea spray drifted high above the sands below, the haziness reaching the buildings in the distance.

"Aye that bunch of buildings is surrounded by water," Jock said. "But they sure ain't golden."

"The lights, Jock." Gertrude shook her head.

Jock raised his fuzzy eyebrows and then rubbed his paws together. "Brrrr, it's a mite chilly, that Cockflincher had a good idea; I wish I had a sporran ta stuff down there to warm me caber. Canna wait to find somethin' dry. I hate water."

"We *all* hate water," Spanky said.

"Catch." Manx threw the TomTom to Jock.

Jock took it and grinned and nodded to him as he turned to follow the others.

Manx stood there on the ridge and watched them walk on; Momma and Rani, Maggie and Spanky, Gertrude, the Major and the rest of the tribe. The city lights seemed alluring; he wondered how they built the immense bridge, the wide pylons; waves smashing and breaking around them, yet holding fast.

He turned to see the outline of his Interceptor in the setting sun, the water lapping the sides of the wrecked vehicles below. Images of his family returned and he blinked hard. He took in a deep breath of salty air and kicked the sand, noticing how knotted it was by grass and thinking he had not seen grass in a long time. And then he turned to see the black shapes of the distant desert they had so precariously crossed, and thought how Simmons had died for nothing.

"...and the people there have to take us in; they have to," Momma said to Rani.

"We still have weapons," Rani said flatly, "but I bet Maggie's pissed at losing her Intratec."

"So not," Maggie replied as she gripped Spanky's paw.

"I don't want to use force anymore," Momma said flatly.

The others nodded.

"Where's Manx?" Maggie suddenly asked.

Rani swung about and looked back past the survivors, into the shadows and grassy slopes, and into the faint outlines of the ridge and escarpment beyond.

Manx was gone.

-- The End --

www.ingramcontent.com/pod-product-compliance
Lightning Source LLC
Chambersburg PA
CBHW020128180626
46810CB00004B/1461